THE WING FITTER AND THE SOUL BINDER

The Wing Fitter and the Soul Binder

Lukas Allen

Lukas Allen

Contents

1

Wing Fitting

Welcome to Heaven.

1

I name you, Tom, a wing fitter.

"What's that again?" I asked.

It's an angel that finds other angels jobs. No matter what, you will fit them the exact wings they need.

"...What if I was an angel of music? I'm great at guitar and-"

Sorry, Tom. This job is perfect for you, and I know it. How do you think I got this job, eh? I found other angels the best jobs they could get.

"...I thought you were God."

Sorry. Nope! I'm just a lowly herald angel.

"...You can't pull any strings for me? Seriously, just listen to me play-"

Enjoy the new gig! We'll start you off in the Departments of Wings and Vehicles, the DWV, where they fit people with wings, under a kind chap named Maximus. He should be able to set you straight.

And poof, the cloud underneath me dissipated, and I fell in Heaven, free fallin' through the sky.

It was like skydiving, but it felt safe.

It was like falling in Heaven, to Heaven, from Heaven.

I still screamed as if my life depended on it, even though I was dead.

The great, wide open, blue sky beckoned me, and I saw an approaching cloud welcome me into its fluffy embrace.

I landed straight through the ceiling of the DWV.

It didn't hurt a bit.

There were all sorts of happy people without wings here, and they greeted me hello.

A big, burly man with just the best angelic wings helped me up from the rubble. I dusted myself off, and noticed the hole in the ceiling was fixed as soon as I blinked up at it.

The man said, "Ho there, man. Did you take a wrong turn at the gate?"

I said, "No, I'm Tom. I'm supposed to work as a wing fitter with you."

I then shook his hand, and the man could crush steel with just his grip.

"Maximus. We always need new interns! This will be grand. I'll set you up with Belladonna. I'll be on break. I'm going out to lunch with my wife! We're so happy we can all live in Heaven in peace." Maximus said.

The man rushed out the doors, as I said, "Intern…? Wait, what?"

Maximus didn't seem to hear me, and met a stunning woman with wings that looked like flower petals in the lobby who hugged the big man gently.

The two left the building and flew off into the sky, and I was left alone.

I heard the cough of someone looking at me.

I turned to look, and saw a grungy looking goth chick looking at me from a doorway.

"Well. C'mon, let me get you to your office. I'm Belladonna, and I'll be your overseer. Deal with it." the woman said. She had giant, trailing, purple wings, like a large bird's, on her back.

I followed the woman, as she coughed again. I asked her, "Are you sick? I thought we were dead already."

Belladonna said, "I just like coughing. *Deal with it.* You'll be in charge of-"

"Giving the other angels their wings, right?" I said.

"Sorry, no. You'll be like a seamstress, stitching wings together for someone who would (ha!) want them. Here's your 'office.' You get off at eight, so get to work." Belladonna said.

"I'm really not that great at sewing..." I said.

"Do I have to do everything?! Fine. Watch me, and you'll get the hang of it soon. I'll sew *one* wing for you, and you can work on the other one. Fucking pitiful excuse for angels these days..." Belladonna muttered, and I sat beside her in the cramped office and watched her sew up a wing.

I hoped to God I didn't have to do this for the rest of my afterlife. This was supposed to be Heaven, for God's sake! I vowed, at least to myself, that I would better my lot in the afterlife, and get that damned herald angel, someday.

2

She stitched up the wing in a matter of minutes. It was beautiful, gorgeous, and so soft. It looked like something any cherubim would be blessed to wear, and be proud of it.

I asked her, as she was sewing the finishing touches, "So how'd you bite it?"

"My own business. Really. I was an organ seller, and after I sold off the extra bit of liver of mine I took it too hard with the booze, y'know celebrating with all the extra cash, and my body couldn't take it and I keeled over." Belladonna said.

"...And you still ended up here? Isn't organ selling illegal?" I asked.

"Yeah, so? Deal with it. They always need organs down below, so I was practically a saint. I just got paid for it, too. How'd *you* die, long-hair?" she said.

"I don't really want to talk about it..." I said.

"Suits me. Some angels get sooo caught up with their deaths, they don't even realize they're literally flying in Heaven now. Whelp, work on the wings, and we'll see if I can (ha!) find some use for them." she said, and sauntered out of the tiny, cramped office.

I tried to sew a wing together, but I'd keep pricking my thumb.

It was going well, I think, after a long time of copying what Belladonna did, then I noticed I made two left wings.

My makeshift wing could maybe hold up in Heaven, but it probably couldn't last against any sort of strong breeze...

I sighed, and began remaking the wing-

Belladonna came in, and said, "We need two wings, stat. Hand 'em over, and we'll set the new saint up with his pair! Gonna be so much fun, seeing him fly. I think this guy is actually credited with world peace, or something like that."

Belladonna snatched up my wings before I could protest, and I followed her out the door telling her I wasn't finished.

She ignored me, and attached the wings to a happy, joyful man in a back room, just put them on his back, and poof, they were attached.

The man whooped in glee, and said, "This is what I wanted for the Earth my entire life! I'm so happy I too can experience this bliss. We all deserve peace."

Belladonna said, "Care to try them out? Let's go out back to the yard, and let you fly!"

The man nodded quickly, and I kept silent.

The man waited for the gentle breeze to go past, as he was crouched for liftoff, and jumped into the air, and flew.

I opened my eyes from the disaster I was sure was going to take place, and saw the saint flying... to the right in a circle.

He was whooping and dancing in the air, all to the right, and Belladonna was cheering for him as he flew.

The saint flew down, well, tried to, but veered off to the left of us too far.

He ran up to us, and said, "I'm so happy!! This is amazing!! Thank you so much!"

Belladonna said, "You're welcome, new saint. Enjoy your Paradise! Go on, shoo!"

The saint smiled at her, and flew off to the right in the sky of Heaven.

3

Maximus came back, and I was about to stitch up a new pair of wings again. I grumbled to myself why literal Heaven had to be like a normal day at a new, crappy job, but was thankful no one noticed my mistake, at least.

Maximus called me into his office, and said, "What do you suppose Cass needs, Tom?"

The smiling, platinum blonde haired woman looked at me hopefully, hands clasped together, and I said to her, "...Er, what kind of wings do you want?"

She said, "I want something pretty and pink."

Maximus said, "I think we're actually out of pink feathers currently, but don't fear! I'll call in a favor."

Maximus then snapped his fingers, and I looked in surprise as pink, sparkly, pretty wings appeared on the woman's back.

The woman looked back at her wings, gasped, and said, "SPARKLES! I forgot about sparkles!! They're like every good birthday card I've ever gotten!! Thank you so much!"

She smiled in glee, and hugged Maximus close, then went out the doors, waving at us, to go explore her afterlife some more.

I asked Maximus, ignoring the fact that it was so easy for him to fit someone with the perfect wings, "...Um, how come I don't have wings?"

"Hm? I thought you didn't want any. They're not really necessary, actually." Maximus said.

"...Can I have something that's golden?" I asked.

Maximus sighed, and said, "If that's your choice. The only other golden winged angel I know of was Lucifer. But some people do try to make the gold wings fashionable again."

I said, "...Um, no thanks, then. Can't I… What's the best wings?"

"There are no best wings. Every wingspan, wing color, or wing composition is equal in Heaven's eyes." Maximus said.

"...Then this is like a car dealership, where the owner says every car is equal… C'mon, man, at least tell me which wings get the most mileage." I said.

Maximus sighed, and said, "Listen, howbout you go and spend the rest of day with one of my friends. He should be able to show you, no matter what, you can do astounding things, whether you are big or small, courageous or meek, or what wings you have. His name is Scott, and he's an angel of kindness. Learning from him should give you some Heavenly insight. You'll be the best wing fitter in all the afterlife after these lessons, I guarantee it."

Maximus called Scott up on his phone, and I wondered about the technology of Heaven.

Did it just copy the living world? Or was it just something to make certain angels feel at home, and not really necessary? What was the point of a phone, when I saw the man fly down already, on tiny wings, and greet Maximus at the door?

I shook Scott's hand, and I introduced myself to him as Tom.

4

Scott and I walked down the streets of Heaven, him with his tiny wings and me with... no wings.

The first thing we did was go into a gas station and get some soda, free of charge of course. The cashier was the most buoyant, cheerful person I've ever met, and I don't think I'd meet another person like her. Her wings were rainbow colored.

Scott and I sat at the curb drinking soda, talking about my past life. It felt strangely really good to talk about the things I never got to do to this person.

We walked down the street some more, and played basketball with a few angels in a scrimmage. Their wings were orange and black, like the basketball's. They trash talked in a very polite way, that actually *did* sound like they were giving each other compliments. One of them explained to me they like to do that with each other to fire each other up. Scott flew twenty feet in the air and slam dunked the ball in the game we played.

We continued to walk down the street, and met an angel smoking on the curb. He looked like he was homeless, and I asked if this was true, but he said, "Whatcha mean? I am always home here." He smiled happily, and offered his cigarette to us, which we each took and inhaled from. He had grey, dirty wings.

Scott said, "So have you figured out what wings you want yet?"

I said, "I have no idea. Everyone here has different wings, and they're all so different themselves. I couldn't bear to be typecast if I chose the wrong wings."

Scott said, "Then don't choose wings. Be like me, and be a man of the people. Flight power is the same no matter what, even if you don't have wings. See, watch this."

Scott then flew in the light breeze, fluttering his teeny tiny wings, and smiled down at me. He swooped back to the street, and told me to try.

I jumped... but landed back on the cloud.

Scott shrugged. He said, "The very first thing we do here is learn to fly. Guess you'll have to do that without wings."

"...But-"

"Listen, we can all fly, believe it or not. Sometimes we just need a little kindness to learn we can. You'll be able to fly, in other ways too if you feel like it." Scott said.

"I know, but-"

"Just take it easy. Do you have a place to sleep? I can set you up at a hotel if you like. Some angels really like it there, as they were in life, constantly traveling from hotel to hotel with no place of their own." Scott said.

"...I think that'd suit me, actually, yeah. I was kinda like that in life." I said.

Scott smiled so kindly to me, and told me to follow him to the hotel. We took the bus there.

Scott said, "So, just checking if you learned anything from me... Have you?"

I said, "...I think so. Be kind. You always seemed to be nice to everyone, without pushing yourself on them. They just accepted you, because you accepted them."

Scott nodded, and said, "Yes. There's so much more to kindness, but so little needs to be remembered. Be kind. That is all. My friend, Ronnie, will see you tomorrow, so goodnight, Tom. Don't worry about the DWV, they can... carry on without you for a while."

I sighed a sigh of relief, and bid him goodnight, going to my comfortable room on the top floor.

I smoked on the balcony, and looked out on Heaven. Gosh... What a sight.

5

I yawned awake. That was *the best* sleep I've ever had. I just had the most pleasant dreams, and I felt *so* refreshed.

I smiled, sang myself a song, got dressed, and went down to breakfast.

There was a man in the lobby with dark black wings, arguing with a server that the bacon wasn't fresh.

The server said, "...Of course it's fresh. It's not even literal bacon, it's Heaven bacon."

The black winged angel said, "That's what I mean!! It's not fresh! In Hell they never had this sort of problem, they killed something, and let you eat it right the fuck away!"

The server said, "...Oh. You're one of those angels. My apologies. Would you like something that's-"

"I want to party with you, my dude. Let's go find my idiot trainee and ditch this dump, get some hookers and floozies and-" the black winged angel said.

The server just shook his head with a smile, and said, "That's not really my afterlife, sir. I just like doing this. The best job I ever had was working at a hotel, and I never feel better than serving people."

The black winged angel said, "Bahhh. Ok, just gimme some booze and I'll hit the road."

"Of course, sir." the server said, and handed the black winged angel a bottle of bourbon.

The black winged angel noticed me as I was getting breakfast, very happy with the bacon that looked so hot, crispy and delicious, and he said, "Oh! You're the wing fitter! Cool. Follow me, chump. The name's Ronnie, previously the King of Hell."

I opened my eyes wide, and said, "King of Hell? Is that even a thing?"

Ronnie said, "Of course it's a thing! Never lasts too long, but it's a nonstop party all throughout! I'd steer clear of it if I was you. C'mon, I'm supposed to teach you how to rock."

I smiled knowingly, and said, "I think I know a thing or two about rocking."

"Do you? Well I bet you've never partied with succubi from the lower abyss, and the Demon of Music himself. C'mon. Don't make me ask you again." he said.

I shrugged, put down my food, and Ronnie passed me the bourbon which I drank from.

We drank breakfast, and I never thought, but desperately hoped, that the alcohol of Heaven would be the best ever.

It was.

I felt happy, I felt sad, remarkably so in all capacity. Ronnie was saying, as he drove the car and drank from the bourbon, "Thing is, I'm an angel of music, dude. And the thing is, music is God's gift. There is nothing better than music, y'know?"

I just nodded, feeling completely safe as Ronnie drove the car completely drunk, completely well, even if very fast.

Ronnie said, "I had a shit ton of problems with music in the living world, but it's a skill like none other. It can bring the best out of us, it can bring the worst. But it sounds so, so right."

I asked him, "How did you get black wings? Are those more evil than gold wings?"

Ronnie said, "My wings are a symbol. A symbol that I've been through the very worst. Hardly any people get out of Hell and then become angels, but those who do have a choice. We can either flaunt our suffering, or forget about it. I chose to flaunt it. Let all see my past suffering, and learn from my Hell."

"Very cool." I said, "I like that you don't hide behind the past, but use it as a shield instead."

"Or a sword. Those young kids I teach, the angels who died young, just can't get enough of the wings... heh. It's a good way to catch their attention, and they take the lessons more to heart." Ronnie said.

"...So you're a teacher?" I asked.

"The best. I'm on my way to school now, to teach the kids who didn't get to grow up or the mute who never got to sing how to make melodies and symphonies. I'll drop you off by Kurt, who wants to teach you some 'real' world knowledge. But one thing... Do you know how to rock now?" Ronnie said.

I smiled, nodded, and said, "Pass on the love, that's how I rock."

"Cool. Glad my lesson wasn't misheard. Peace."

Ronnie stopped before a man in a ratty sweater, lounging on a cloud floating above the street. I took one more swig of bourbon that Ronnie offered, then got out. Ronnie sped away laughing a demonic laugh.

6

The man on the cloud gently floated down to me, and shook my hand, introducing himself as Kurt. He had pretty classic angel wings. He gave me a phone, and said, "Oh. If you ever need to talk to any of us, bounce off any queries you might have, here's a prayer phone."

"...Prayer phone?" I said.

"Yeah. It's also really handy if, y'know, you need to answer a prayer. I use it all the time in my job as an angel of suicide prevention." Kurt said, smiling comfortably.

"...Sounds like a difficult job! How do you do that again?" I said.

Kurt and I walked through the clouds, jumping onto and off them here and there through the skies of Heaven, and Kurt said, "It's a tough gig, I'll say that. I, y'know, make people not want to kill themselves. This can be done in many ways, but only the right way will suit. I get a lot of help from other angels in my job, so just know, there's no shame in asking for help."

We got to a plateau of clouds, and sat on it for a bit, enjoying the view.

Kurt got a call on his prayer phone, and he answered, listening to the prayer.

I heard a man say on Kurt's prayer phone, "...Please. Help me. Please, God... I want to kill myself, I don't know what to do... I feel trapped, endlessly so. I don't know what to do… I'm going to kill myself by taking all my medication, and slicing my wrists. Is anyone listening? Are you there, God?"

Kurt took my hand immediately and we jumped off the cloud plateau, falling to a low cloud looking down at someone on a bench in a park, praying to the sky.

The man below us was crying gently, looking straight at us.

"...Can he see us?" I asked.

"No, but he might be able to feel that we are with him. Now watch closely." Kurt said.

Kurt jumped off the cloud, landing beside the man, and walked beside the man as he shuffled home.

My cloud followed them, and Kurt bumped into a lady who was walking her dog.

The dog sniffed at Kurt as Kurt pet him, but instead the dog spent more attention on the man, licking at the man's knees.

The woman said, "Oh, I'm sorry, he does that sometimes. He's a licker!"

The man said to the woman, "Oh, it's alright. I love dogs." He said to the dog, "You're a cutie, aren't'cha you little pupper…" and pet the dog.

The woman looked inquisitively at the man, and said, "My name's Shauna. My dog is Jerry. You ok? You don't look like you're feeling too well."

The man said, "My name's Rico. I'm fine, I just… I'm fine. Well, I should be going. It was nice meeting you and your dog."

Shauna waved Rico goodbye, and Rico didn't shuffle anymore, but walked slowly home, smiling slightly to himself.

Kurt jumped back up to the cloud I was on, and I said, "...That's it? But… won't that man kill himself?"

Kurt smiled, and said, "I'll be watching over him for a while, but I don't think so. He's gonna be wanting to see Shauna and Jerry again soon, so he'll push on for a bit longer."

"Subtle. I liked that you gave that man a chance to live in a smaller way, like giving him a rope to pull himself up, instead of carrying him." I said.

"Not all cases are like that, and sometimes... I have failed. I can't stomach death. Can you?" he said.

I shook my head.

Kurt said, "Well, I'll tell Max to take it easy on you. He's an angel of death, and he'll pick you up... right about now. That's him, in the pale car. We work pretty closely sometimes. Have you learned anything, Tom?"

I said, "Life can be lived in slight ways, not only in grand events... and that you can always keep living."

Kurt smiled, and said, "Good. Well, peace. I've got a long day, and that guy was the easy part. Later."

A pale car flew to our cloud, and a short angel with normal wings waved me in as Kurt got another call on his prayer phone.

7

Max, the angel of death, said, "You can't always keep living. Sometimes... people die, and there's nothing anyone can do about it."

"...Not even God?" I said.

"Life is a blessing, a gift, but on a timeframe. It ends, but the end is not a final end. The end is just a doorway to the next life, our afterlife, in Heaven. Let me pick up some people, and you'll see for yourself." Max said.

"...You're not going to kill them, are you?"

Max laughed, and said, "No. These people died from a random accident, a car crash that ended fatally. There they are, looking confused at their past bodies."

Max flew the car down... to a grisly accident. I felt faint looking at the bits and pieces scattered on the street. There were two people, ghosts, a man and a woman, arguing about their cars still.

"Well, look, you totaled my truck with that SUV, and I deserve some sort of restitution for that!" the man said.

"Truck?? Look at my body! The cops can't even tell that's me, besides looking at my wallet!!" the woman said.

Max came up to the two as I watched from the passenger seat of the car, and the man said, "Oh great. An angel. Proof that I'm dead. Whelp, take me to Heaven, and I can get this broad off my back..."

The woman said, "Me first! This guy obviously belongs in Hell, the way he drives!"

Max said, "You're both not going to Heaven."

The pair were silent, mouths agape.

Max said, "...Oh! I didn't mean you're going to Hell. You both have to make up for some things before you can be accepted to Heaven, so I'm going to be dropping you off at Purgatory. I'll be your angel of death on the drive. I'm Max, pleased to meet you."

Max shook their hands, as the two grumbled, but the two got in the pale car as Max did, and Max started up his car and drove up.

The two in the back started to argue some more, but as soon as we got through the clouds to the sky above, they gasped, looking on at the beauty. I smiled to myself. Seeing this sight for the first time wowed me too.

We got to... a strange place. A big park, somehow in the afterlife, and Max said, "This is Purgatory, and that's Paul over there, guy with the slashes on his face and the dark coat. He's a caretaker of Purgatory, and he'll get you all straightened out."

The woman said, "I'm scared."

The man said, "Me too."

Max turned back to them, and said, "I know. It won't be so bad. Think of it like taking a bath before putting on clothes, which I assure you are nice, clean clothes in Heaven."

The two sighed in relief, and thanked Max for being so gentle with them as their angel of death.

Max smiled at them as they got out, and Max said to me, "So. Whatcha learn?"

I looked at him quizzically, and said, "...I'm not sure. I think just not to die, but I already messed that up."

Max laughed, and said, "I'd say the most important part of life is to cherish it, before it's gone for good. But don't think about it too hard. Not everything needs to be a grand lesson. Ready to hang out with Paul?"

"Sure. Thanks for the drive, Max." I said, and shook his hand, then got out of the car. Max flew back down to Earth, an angel of death, as busy as ever.

8

I walked up to the man with the scars on his face, with the pair who got in an accident, as he looked up at the sky. He had the brightest white wings I had ever seen. He said to us, "Hey there. I'm Paul. I'll be helping you guys through Purgatory. It's a blast, really."

I said, "Oh, I'm not with them. I just came to learn. My name's Tom."

Paul said, "Then you're here to go through Purgatory. Anything you guys want to confess right off the bat?"

The woman said, "He hit me with his truck!"

The man said, "She ran a red light!"

Paul looked at the two with a quizzical expression on his face, and said, "Ok. Then I want you both to start off by saying sorry to the other."

The pair grumbled, but mumbled their apologies to each other.

Paul smiled happily, and said, "That's better. Probably feels like a big weight is off your chest, eh?"

The woman said, "...Um... I guess..."

The man said, "...Sure... kinda..."

Paul looked at me, expecting me to say a sin, and I looked at him in surprise. I said, "...I'm not really sure what I need to confess. There's a few things, but... Didn't I already go to Heaven?"

Paul smiled gently, and said, "Purgatory is not a damnation, or even a lesson on what you did wrong in life. It is a chance to get that weight of sin off of your chest, and feel good again. I thought it was marvelous, my first time here, and kept at it in the afterlife. I was nearly damned for my sins, amongst them original sin from my genetic father's evil, but have been forgiven. See? That feels good to say, I own my sin, and I let it go."

The woman said, "As a little girl… I once stole from the donation basket at church…"

Paul said, "Then you are forgiven."

The woman said, "...That's it? Really? That actually was something that drove me away from faith, as I thought I'd be damned forever for it."

The man huffed, and said, "That's nothing. I cheated on my wife. Now forgive me for *that...*"

Paul said, "I think I have a better idea. She should be asleep and dreaming… and…. There she is, right now." Paul looked off into the horizon, and a woman wandered through Purgatory to us.

"Ch-Chelsea? CHELSEA!" the man said, and ran to the woman, picking her up in a hug.

"Dave?? I'm so happy to- to-" the wife, Chelsea, said, and burst out crying in her husband's arms.

The husband, Dave, said, "A-Are you d-dead?? Please don't be dead."

Chelsea said, "No. But you are. I got the news, and it felt like my life ended, too. I'm so sorry…"

Dave said, "I-I'm sorry too. I miss you, and love you. I hope we'll see eachother soon- Sometime again."

Chelsea said, "I love you too, Dave. Is this Heaven? It must be Heaven."

Dave said, "...This is Purgatory. I have a few sins to get through, then I'll be playing golf with God. I need to say- I'm sorry for my unfaithfulness in our marriage. It was a mistake that ruined my life."

Chelsea let out a half laugh, and said, "That's all? I'm more angry you're not going to be around to watch the kids grow up... I forgive you."

The two smiled at each other, and we watched as they kissed, and Chelsea woke up, disappearing from Purgatory.

Dave sighed, walked back over to us with tears in his eyes, and said, "Thank you, Paul."

The woman that Dave got in a car crash with said, "...My name's Denise, Dave. Let's get through this together, ok?"

Dave said, "Sounds good, Denise."

I finally said to Paul, "I have some things I want to confess."

9

I met St. Peter at the gates of Heaven again, and he let all three of us into Heaven, as we waved goodbye to Paul, who had more work to do in Purgatory.

I got a message from a courier angel, who was the fastest I've ever seen fly, to an invitation to a ball in God's honor.

God is going to be there?? Gosh, how could I refuse?

I went to get dressed up in a suit, custom made for me on demand in moments, and took the bus to the ball, which I nodded to the bus driver again. The ball was taking place in the grand house of St. Valentine's, where everyone he could invite could show up if they wanted.

I expected all of Heaven to be there, but it actually looked like an average amount of people showed up, average for the huge ball that was going to take place.

I saw all sorts of fantastic, beautiful people. I saw a blind man being escorted by a tiger, I saw holy people from ages past, some in long white robes, and others in fashion of modern times. I saw the seraphim fly above us in the sky, waving down happily to us. I guess they were the security or something? I wasn't really sure, but they sure made me feel safe.

I squinted at a man chatting politely with one of these seraphim, the seraph an albino woman who had six wings of white fire. That bastard...

I went up to the man, and said, "You're that herald angel that stuck me with the wing fitter job."

He turned to me, smiled, and said, "That I did. Fits, don't it?"

"...How come your voice isn't booming bold like before?" I asked.

"Oh! That's just a trick I like to do sometimes. Pretty neat, eh? **The herald speaketh, God is approaching.**"

"Yeah, yeah, cut it out. I've got a grudge with you-"

"No, really. He just passed right behind you. Shame to miss someone like that..." the herald angel said.

I quickly turned around behind me, looking for God, so I can at least take up my grievances about this job to the big man himself, but I didn't see anyone behind me who looked remotely like how I pictured God, even though they were all fantastic looking people of all diversity.

The seraph placed a hand on my shoulder, turning me back to them, and she said, "You'll get another chance. God prefers to find you, half the time. But seek and you shall find, and all that."

I slumped my shoulders and frowned at this beautiful seraph woman. She was wearing a white dress that didn't contrast with her albino white skin.

The herald angel said, "Tom, this is Yule. She's a seraph, protecting God's throne, God's creation, and all of God's people."

I shook Yule's hand, and she nodded her head at me. She said, "I used to be an angel of war, but after I was promoted we decided to cut down that department. We don't need *any* war, even God's peaceful one, especially now that we have world peace down below and Hell is sealed for good. Please, come inside, Tom. I'm going to make sure everyone we could get got here on time. Scott is going to sing for us! Gonna be swell."

I nodded to Yule, squinted at the herald angel who continued to smile at me, and went inside.

10

Wow. Scott, the angel of kindness, sure could sing. I wondered why *he* wasn't the angel of music. He sang Hallelujah for us, and we all clapped for him when he finished, all of us cheering.

A band came out, and played dance music for us, real, live performers, and everyone danced and partied with each other.

I went to get some more punch, which tasted like alcoholic bliss, and bumped into a blonde angelic woman with cute, black wings. She had a cross tattoo on her exposed chest.

She accidentally spilled my punch all over my suit, and she said, "Oh! My bad. Watch where you're going next time! Care to dance?"

She smiled so sweetly, and I instantly forgave her for bumping into me, in fact I thanked God for it.

We danced, over and over, one last time. The last one we said, then the last one, and the last one.

We took a break and talked, laughing and joking. She was such a fun woman! I finally introduced myself, after we finally caught our breaths again from dancing and laughing.

She said, "You're a wing fitter? That's so cool! We all need a little help finding out who we want to be. I'm Mary Jane, and I'm an angel of Hell. Call me Jane."

I blinked, and said, "...Real Hell? What are you doing in Heaven, then?"

Jane said, "Well, Hell's where I come from. I was raised there. The angel of Hell thing is really just a title, but it shows that I've been through the worst, and will help others through their worst in any way possible."

I said, "...Oh! What did you do to get stuck in Hell? If you don't mind me asking. I thought children didn't go to Hell."

Jane sighed, looking around the room with a smile, looked back at me and said, "My father is the Devil, Tom."

I blinked, looked into her eyes as she smiled nicely at me... and I knew she was speaking the truth.

I instantly went a little pale despite myself. I had been dancing with the Devil's Daughter, Mary Jane.

Jane said, "Oh, quit the look. I usually don't tell anyone about that anymore, but it's my past. Least I can do is own it."

"Sorry. This is all kind of new to me, being in Heaven and all that. I don't really know where I was before I got here... felt like I was simply dreaming, or something." I said.

"Some people do that, and it takes them a long time to actually find the afterlife after they've died. Well, I'm going to go before JC gets here. He always gets so mushy sometimes, but you know God..." she said, rolling her eyes.

I said, before she walked away, "Will I ever see you again?"

She turned back, smiled, and said, "When you're in the worst moment of your life, I'll be there, and things won't feel so bad. I doubt you'll have *any* worst moments these days... so don't get your hopes up."

She winked at me, and left the ball.

11

I sighed longingly after Jane, and someone behind me, a woman, said, "Don't chase *that* one, Tom. She's a rockin' woman, for sure, but sometimes she rocks a little too hard..."

I looked behind me, and saw a Japanese woman with the biggest wings I've ever seen, compared to her slight body, standing with a young man in a pink hoodie, sporting white wings with pink accents.

The young man said, "I think they could start something, don't you? What would be the harm?"

The Japanese woman shook her head, and said, "You still have so much to learn, Set... Sometimes love needs to be withdrawn, and not thrown freely at every stranger you meet." She then went up to me, and said, "My name's Nevaeh, Tom. I think I've heard your prayers once or twice."

"...And what kind of angel are you?" I asked.

"Angel of love, at your service." Nevaeh said, and curtsied to me.

I grinned, and said, "Really. That's a pretty good pick up line. Mind if I use it sometime?"

Nevaeh laughed, and said, "I'd remain true to the job you have, and really wouldn't worry about being a wing fitter. Wing fitters help all sorts of people, with-"

The young man, Set, said, "With their wings, their hearts, bodies, minds... You could help the next revolutionary in Heaven figure out how to help people better. I just went to a wing fitter, and she touched up my wings with these beautiful accents! She simply looked to my soul, and found exactly what I always wanted..."

I said, "...So I'm sort of just a wing stylist?"

Nevaeh shrugged, and said, "If that's how you want to direct yourself. How about I tell you a little bit of my job, and you can state what sort of thing I should do to improve it... I was helping this young couple start a romance, and they were happy for a good while, but she got pregnant, he lost his job, and everything is crumbling to bits. This is a hypothetical question, of course, but what do you think I should do?"

I pondered, and asked, "Do they still love each other?"

Nevaeh said, "It comes and goes, usually at the behest of their sexual organs."

"Hmm... Then I would say they can find love elsewhere, since if they are only interested in sex, then they shouldn't stick with a dying relationship. Or at least that's what you should nudge them towards, being an angel of love, and help them find that true love elsewhere. The beginning love is never the last." I said.

"Very wise words." Nevaeh said, "But you forgot about something. Love is not tied to sex. There is a new love, growing in her womb, that will bring them joy they never could achieve. Granted, you are correct that dying relationships shouldn't be clung to for sexual sake, but this couple will continue to have a love even if they separate, they will have the love for this child. Love usually grows when nurtured correctly, so I nudged them to stick with each other at least until the baby's born, and if they still feel like drifting apart, then at least they got to see their child brought into the world together."

I nodded, and said, "I like that. I *did* kind of assume an angel of love only helps with romantic relationships, and didn't think at the start that there is love found in so many other ways."

"Like love for good cooking. I invite you to dinner with my family, Tom. We have a little bit extra food and could use one more mouth to feed. Would you care to join us?" Nevaeh asked.

"...But I really wanted to see God-"

"Nonsense. Come, I'd love to talk with you more about specific scenarios tied to the heart..." Nevaeh said, took me by the arm as I looked back, and I *swore* I thought I saw God take the stage.

Set waved us goodbye, and obstructed my view of God just as I was about to spot him.

12

I shook the big, burly man's, Felix's, hand as he smiled at me. He was Nevaeh's, the angel of love's, husband, and had averagely proportioned wings for his huge frame. He said dinner would be served soon, and we were just waiting for a few other guests.

I watched him use the knife in the kitchen as we listened to the radio, and I've never seen a man that fast at cooking. It was a whirlwind of blades, and then the onions, tomatoes, and meat would be sliced to ribbons.

"What's your job in Heaven, Felix?" I asked him, with Nevaeh and I sitting at the kitchen table.

"That's a tough question to answer, actually." Felix said, "I wanted to be an angel of war, as all my life I had to fight as a gladiator, but I switched it up and became an angel of peace. It's actually a much better job than killing and mutilating, like I did in the arena of the Romans, and is very diverse. There is so much you can apply your life to, in times of peace. Lately I've taken up cooking, and am enjoying it rather much. I'm only a novice, however."

Nevaeh shook her head, sipping at her wine, and said, "You could go toe to toe with any fancy pantsy chef in Heaven. Don't sell yourself short."

Felix smiled at her, and said, "I just wish I knew more about Heavenly materials, or even ingredients from parts of the world I've never been to. Those angels of food know all about that, and I'm meeting one for lunch tomorrow to discuss the finer arts of cooking."

Nevaeh giggled, and said, "Those guys are more for food management and stopping world hunger, rather than cooking. Be prepared to be surprised when you meet this food angel. But still. It's a good goal to shoot for, for the people on Earth, to make every single person healthy, well fed, and in peace."

There was a ring of the doorbell, and Nevaeh went to answer. I asked Felix, "Is it your kids or someone?"

Felix said, "Actually, no. Nevaeh and I never had a chance to reproduce. Have you heard of the barbaric custom of castration of slaves?"

I frowned, and said, "...I think so, in a history book somewhere or something."

"Well. Just know it is a big regret of mine, that I could never carry on my seed. It's one of the biggest regrets of Nevaeh's, as well... She has spent all her life learning and talking of love, with me after we met, and it is still depressing to us knowing that we will never complete love's ultimate goal." Felix said.

I frowned again, and said, "I think people put too much pressure on themselves to make babies. There's lots of other ways to continue your legacy. Like, your cooking. It smells divine already, and I will always remember this meal and your company by the smell of that fresh baked garlic bread and homemade sauce alone. This is in fact a legacy, the memories we inspire in others."

Felix smiled, and said, "That cheers me up, Tom. Go sit, and I'll serve dinner."

I walked into the dining room, smiling, and my smile left as I saw Maximus from the DWV with his wife sit down with us for dinner.

13

"Tom! How are the lessons? I bet you must feel like a professional wing fitter by now!" Maximus said.

I mumbled something about how I'd be kidding myself if I said I was professional at wing fitting, and Nevaeh said to Maximus and his wife, "So nice to see you guys again! How is everything with the garden, Fate?"

Maximus's wife, Fate, an angel with flower petal wings, said, "Booming and bountiful, as always. I love being an angel of nature! Flowers practically spring up to greet me as I pass. Speaking of which… I noticed your tulips need some water."

Nevaeh said, "Aren't they Heaven tulips, though?"

Fate smiled and said, "They still enjoy it, if anything!"

Nevaeh shrugged, and watered the tulips.

Felix set down the food, spaghetti and meatballs with homemade garlic bread and sauce, and I breathed in, and my stomach could've been satisfied with the delectable aroma alone.

We talked about the afterlife and such. I mostly was silent, but happy to be accepted by these people, an angel of peace, an angel of love, an angel of nature, and…

I asked Maximus what kind of angel he actually was. "You're a wing fitter too, right?"

Maximus said, "Actually, no, I'm not. I'm an angel of welcome. It took me so long to be accepted into Heaven, all part of God's plan in actuality, so I took on the job to better help people feel at home here."

I said, "Angel of welcome? Is that really necessary?"

Fate said, "Oh yes. The action of opening your arms in greeting or looking away in distaste can change someone's entire perspective on people or a place."

Maximus said, "Quite true. I wanted nothing to do with battle, as I was a gladiator in my past, like Felix, but I didn't know exactly how to apply my skills I learned in life. All I really had was my knowledge of fighting."

Felix said, "We both were quite lost before Yule found us."

I said, "Yule? That seraph?"

Nevaeh nodded, and said, "She's been exploring a lot more of life and the afterlife lately, so we've been growing apart. Still doesn't mean she's not my best friend in the entire world, but... blessings on her for finding her path."

Maximus said, "Ah yes... I learned a lot about kindness from her. At first my welcome was a shining blade in the sunlight, but I learned it can also be a fantastic handshake, or a friendly hello."

Fate said, "I'm so happy our paths crossed, even if it was in the lowest, darkest abyss, and you welcomed me with open arms as well."

Maximus and Fate held hands, looking deeply into each other's eyes and smiling.

Something was bothering me, so I asked, "...Wait, so if you two, Maximus and Felix, were gladiators, were you two, Fate and Nevaeh, also from those times? Forgive me if I'm wrong, but you seem like you two ladies died yesterday in today's time."

They all laughed, and Nevaeh said, "We... broke the rules, a little bit, here and there. Fell in love with angels from Heaven, saved each other from Hell, all that. But that's a different story altogether. I'd ask Yule sometime if you really want to know more about those days."

I nodded, and the conversation changed into one about talking cats, for some odd reason.

14

I went to sleep in the hotel again, and I had an odd dream.

In it a blind woman with black hair was feeling my face in a blank, white room.

She said, "I think a demon of suffering would fit your job qualifications, based on your features."

"D-Demon of suffering??" I said, aghast.

She smiled, looking at me but not directly with those blind eyes, and said, "Well, duh! You've never suffered a day in your life! Your skin is like a newborn babe's! You should be able to help all sorts of demons learn that suffering is really quite unhealthy."

Confused, I said, "...I'm not sure what to make of this. Where am I?"

"Hell. This is the greeting part of my *fantastic* domain. My name's Hanatrix, and I am Hell's mighty and all powerful Queen. Don't let that intimidate you, I also love a good party and love teaching the new demons how to dance!" the blind woman said, smiling.

"...I'm in Hell?! Wait- I was doing so well in Heaven! I swear I'll be a better wing fitter, I promise!!" I stuttered.

Hanatrix looked at me, and gasped, "OH! My apologies. I thought you were unclaimed. Well, Beleth, send him back up, this guy is probably happy enough as it is."

A demon came into the white room, scowled at me, and said to Hanatrix, *"But... Are you sure? Can't we just steal his soul forever and ever, like in the olden days?"*

Hanatrix shook her head, and said, "No, no, no, Beleth... As your commanding Queen I know what I'm doing. Took forever for my mom to get things up to this point, and I've got a policy here. We only take souls who are tired of Heaven, or souls that don't have anywhere else to go. Sorry, Tom. You probably would love to meet all the *fantastic* horrible murderers, rapists, thieves, politicians, lawyers, and scum like that here, but you should stick where you feel like you belong."

I stuttered, "I th-thought Satan ruled Hell."

Hanatrix said, "A common misconception. Satan was sent to Hell, but doesn't always rule it. I like him trapped in a burning book for now, he's so funny at times! Well, remember my offer of demon of suffering! You could really make waves here!"

"...I think I've suffered enough." I said.

Hanatrix winked with a blind eye, and said, "That's what you think. Peace, Tom!"

And she snapped her fingers, and I woke up from my bed in the hotel with a gasp, drenched in sweat.

15

Maximus suggested to me in a phone call, after I asked if I really had to go back to work in the DWV, to go learn from another wing fitter themself. He set up a meeting with a nice woman named Cherry, and I was walking down the street to her address.

Hmm. The road stopped here at some heavenly woods, but the address said it was another block down...

I shrugged, and walked into the forest.

I was amazed at the wildlife that came to greet me. Beautiful butterflies in a clearing, deer, moose, cardinals, were watching me in peace, and there was even a lion sunbathing on a rock, in complete comfortness.

I felt so great, walking down this forest path, with the sun shining brilliantly down on me. I had wondered if animals went to Heaven, and I was pleased to know that they did.

I saw the cabin nestled between two trees, and before I could walk up to it and knock on the door, two *huge* dogs came running up to me and barking something fierce.

I froze. Dogs were good in Heaven, right?

They were.

The dogs immediately played with me, whining and wanting to get pet, getting me all slobbery after one knocked me over in playfulness. I laughed like I was a kid again, and played with these great animals.

"Tuba! Flute! Cut that out..." a sunny looking woman said, who had colorful red wings, like a macaw's, on her back. She helped me back up, and I gave the dogs a last bit of petting, and I introduced myself to the woman.

"I'm Tom. Are you Cherry, the wing fitter?" I said, still smiling from the dogs.

"I am. Based on that handshake... I'd say you're an angel of music! I can tell you can play guitar masterfully by the feeling in your fingers, and your voice is so honed... Yep, gotta be an angel of music. What did you want to see me for again?" she said.

I stopped smiling and said, "Drat! I *knew* that herald angel fudged up my job! He named me a wing fitter!"

Cherry looked surprised, and said, "...Erhem. Wing fitter? Well, I *suppose*... with a few lifetimes of lessons and training... And don't get me started on that new herald angel! He gives a *few* angels jobs they learn to like, and thinks he can do so with whoever he pleases! I've been getting angels the right jobs for millenia now, and it's not always so easy as all that!"

I huffed, and said, "Yeah... I just don't get why God lets that guy do the bold booming voice..."

Cherry smiled, and said, "No matter. Would you like to come in for tea? I haven't had company in a long time, prefer the woods you see, and I'd love to grace someone with my hospitality."

I accepted, and walked into her cabin with her, trailed by the two dogs, Tuba and Flute.

I said to her, sipping the steaming hot tea, "I noticed animals don't have wings like human angels. Why is that?"

She said, "For the longest time, all of our existence practically, humanity has yearned for the skies, for the open air, for quite frankly what we can't have. God just granted our wish, after we have been done living as flightless chimps. But here's the thing... animals, the ones who don't have wings, *know* they don't need wings to get what they want. If you tried to fit a dog with wings, the dog is just going to look at you like you're crazy. Humans are a little more complex with our wishes and desires, and that can be hindering at times."

"Interesting." I said, sipping on my tea, "I do get kind of jealous seeing those angels flap around, blissfully without a care in the world..."

"Oh? You don't know how to fly yet? You never needed wings. See, watch Tuba." Cherry said, and threw a dog treat into the air, which the dog flew up to, even without wings, and snacked on the treat.

"Amazing. Could you teach me to fly? Just without the dog treat." I said, smiling.

Cherry said, "Of course. Let's go find a nice takeoff spot, and you'll learn to fly."

We got to a sunny clearing, and I tried hopping, I tried jumping high, I even tried leaping.

Cherry said, "Think light as air! You can do it, I know it!"

I leapt again and again into the air, and looked at Cherry and said, "I don't know about this, Cherry! What if you just fit me with the wings I need?"

Cherry shook her head, and said, "No! I know you can do this! Don't give up so easily!"

I sighed, jumped one more time, but my prayer phone started ringing as I was in midair.

"You're doing it!" Cherry said.

My prayer phone continued to ring, and I landed on my butt in the grass.

I said to Cherry I had to take this call, after I saw who it was from the caller id.

I answered a prayer.

"I... I miss you, Tom. Your time was too short, and we all miss you. I hope you're in Heaven with the good boys and girls, and the happy doggies and kitties, with all the best food you could ever eat. I love you, Tom. Please... Keep him safe, God."

I dropped the phone to my side. That was-

I looked up at Cherry, who was looking sadly at me.

She helped me up, and gave me a hug, and I hugged her close, very sad.

16

I got caught in the rain on my walk back to town. It sure was storming, for the nice sunny day it was an hour ago.

I had agreed to meet Cherry again for more training as a wing fitter, even though she said she'd have a sharp conversation with that herald angel for me, and try to get God to get me a better job (preferably as an angel of music.)

It was a storm of ages. I feared I'd be blown out of the clouds themself...

And then I was picked up in a strong breeze, and launched into the sky.

I yelped, flying off the clouds and to the open sky.

But someone grabbed me before I could fall to nothingness.

He flew me to town, me safe in his arms, and let me go at the gas station, where I saw a motorcycle parked out front.

The man looked at me, nodded, and went to his motorcycle.

I ran up to him thanking him for saving my life- or something.

The man looked back at me, and said, "No problem. It's what I do. I'm a guardian angel."

The man had the coolest white wings, that just seemed to... I don't know. I'd say they improved his image, but maybe his image improved the wings.

"I'm Tom, a wing fitter. Thanks." I said, offering a hand to shake. The man shook my hand.

He said, "I'm Matt. I'm on my way to the next town. Do you need a lift? It's nice rambling wherever you like, in Heaven."

I thought about it. It would be nice to roam Heaven, rambling free...

I declined, saying, "I think I'm meeting some great people in this part of Heaven, and if I left... It'd just leave their stories half finished, y'know? Thank you for the offer. When I get a bike again I'll take you up on it."

Matt smiled, and said, "Careful on these death traps. I lost my life riding one, but I'm glad I still get to ride. See ya, Tom. We always need more guardian angels, so think of that as a job if you ever get tired of wing fitting."

I smiled, and waved him goodbye, him driving off into the sunshine that opened up from the clouds, the rain parting.

I sat on a bench in front of the gas station, and the cashier with the rainbow wings came out and said, "Oh! I remember you! You're the cool dude with the other cool dude! Whatcha doing out here?"

I looked back at the sky, and said, "Enjoying that. Care to join me?"

She sat beside me, and we looked at the millions, trillions of rainbows draping Heaven's sky. I thought the storm was a bad omen, but you only get rainbows after it has been raining.

17

I was whistling home to the hotel, and I noticed someone was copying my whistling behind me.

I looked behind me. No one there.

I continued whistling, and the whistler took up the rhythm as I whistled the melody.

I stopped whistling. I looked behind me. No one there.

I squinted at a bush... I went behind it, and shouted, "Ah HA...! Oh. No one there..."

I shrugged, and continued walking.

The whistling came from above me, and I looked up.

There was a dark woman with big, yellow, canary wings on her back, whistling down at me and flying in a circle.

I crossed my arms looking at her, smiled, and said, "Hey now, why don't you come down from there and whistle at me face to face?"

She hovered in the air in front of me, and gave a sharp whistle, WEeeeeHEW.

She landed in front of me, stuck her hands on her hips, and said, "Whatcha doin' whistlin' without wings? You're like an ostrich on legs!"

I shrugged, and said, "I hear they're not really necessary, at least not for whistling!" I then gave a sharp whistle back, HEWeeeeEE.

She giggled, and said, "My name's Holly. I'm a finder angel, and I found you!"

I looked at her quizzically, and said, "My name's Tom, and I'm a wing fitter. I thought I found you? What are you finding me for, anyway?"

She shrugged, saying, "Who knows! But I found ya!"

"Hmm..." I hmmed, "Can you find me a better job? I'm not sure about this whole wing fitting thing..."

She said, "Oh! Let's go look at that hotdog stand! I'm sure they must have all sorts of jobs available!"

I followed her as she flew down the street, and she swooped down to the hot dog stand, asking if there were any jobs available for me. The hot dog stand man had checkered angel wings.

The hot dog stand owner said, "Of course! Most people hate this job, but I find so many new people, every day, serving hot dogs!"

Holly said, "There ya go! We'll also find two premium, Chicago style hot dogs, please!"

But something was bothering me. I said to him, "It looks like your wing is just a little off... Mind if I look at it?"

He turned his back to me, and I slightly readjusted the right wing to align with the left. I'm not really sure how I did it, but it seemed in a way really easy to do.

The hot dog owner flapped his wings, and said, "By God... I don't know... I feel... balanced? I usually never use my wings! Cool! Thank you, sir! You oughta be a wing fitter, or something!"

I smiled, as he handed us our hot dogs, and I said I'll take his words under advisement. Holly and I ate our hot dogs, (delicious, filled with toppings, an orgasm of flavor,) and she said, "So! If you ever need anything else found, I'm your gal! Call me! I'm the Holly with the canary wings!"

I nodded to her, and she flew down the street, whistling in the air on canary wings.

I hoped I'd find a purpose to my afterlife, someday. Who knows? Maybe finding this wing fitter job wasn't that bad.

18

I was walking back to Cherry's for more lessons, when I heard a familiar, booming bold voice in the forest. He said, **"So that's the trick, Rasputin. Pretty neat, eh?"**

And then another voice said, "Simple. I wouldn't overuse it, in case the effect gets worn down."

I peeked out from a tree, and saw the herald angel talking to a black and grey cat.

He was petting the cat a little roughly, but the cat was responding well to the pets, and rubbing against his legs as he sat on a large stone.

Wait. Did that cat just talk?

I walked out to meet him, ready to shout and complain and all sorts of angry bits... but he looked at me so kindly, and I... I just forgot what I was going to say.

I finally noticed his wings. They were wings on his back like an eagle's, and he floofed them out for me.

He said, "Howdy, Tom. What are you doing in the forests o' Heaven? I've just been talking to my good friend, Rasputin, the cat."

The black and grey cat mewled up at me, and rubbed against my legs.

I reached down and pet him as he purred.

The little cat made me smile, and I felt like he was accepting me, same as this herald angel did, in a strange way. I turned to the herald angel and said, "Thanks for giving me somewhere to start. I don't know how I'll *ever* be a good wing fitter, but I can try."

The herald angel said, "Well, I've been hearing all sorts of good things about you! I wasn't about to set you on a task and then leave you to the wolves. I checked in, here and there. Why don't you start up a wing fitter office, if the job is still interesting to you? I'm sure anyone you've met would be pleased to start up the occupation with you."

I rubbed my chin, and said, "Hmm. I'd need someone to make the wings, find the materials and people, and even teach me more about how to find that perfect job for everyone... Oh! I know! I could get Belladonna to sew, Holly to find people and materials, and Cherry could be my mentor. I know a little bit how to position the wings right, and I'm a little nervous... but actually, this is kind of exciting!"

The herald angel smiled, and said, "Glad I could help. Oh, did you still want to see God? I can probably schedule a meeting with him if you still want."

I said, "I think I would like that. I'd love to thank him personally for the opportunity to live in Paradise. It really is a dream come true."

The herald angel bowed to someone behind me, and said, "Then I wouldn't keep Him waiting."

I slowly looked behind me, and I met God.

2

Soul Binding

But deep in the heartless abyss of Hell, a new soul was waking up from a pleasant nap...

19

"Wait... You mean she's just a normal person? What's she doing here?"

"Don't ask me! Just because I'm Queen of Hell doesn't mean I know all the answers!"

I blinked my eyes open, in a warm, comfy bed-

Oh. That's because the bed was surrounded by lava and flames, as two shadowy figures were talking about me.

I yawned, got out of bed, and hopped over the rocks in the lava to meet them.

They were a black haired, blind woman in the most colorful clothes and even a golden crown on her head, and a... demon.

I shook their hands. So delightful!

The blind woman smiled, y'know kinda at me but not directly, and said, "Oh! She's a positive one! That's good, we could always use more positivity in Hell!"

The demon said, *"I think you, Hanatrix, have enough positivity for all of us..."*

"That's *Queen* Hanatrix to you, Beleth the Butler! Anyway, how did you end up here, miss? I don't think this has ever happened before!" the blind woman said.

I blinked, and said, "This is a cool dream. I love drawing demons and cool characters like you! Whatcha guys wanna do? Wanna have... a tea party?!?"

The blind woman shrugged at the demon, and the demon shrugged back.

We sat drinking tea, surrounded by fire and scary, scary screams, and I introduced myself as Joli. "Lafaya Joliet Bonaparte, actually, is my full name. But just call me Joli. My parents were really weird!"

The demon said, as he was sipping tea, *"Probably not as weird as their offspring..."*

The blind woman, Hanatrix, nudged the demon, looked at me, and gently said, "...So how do I break this to you nicely... You're dead, Joli."

"Hm? Oh, I die in dreams all the time! That's what makes them fun!" I said, smiling at her even though she couldn't see it.

She smiled back, and said, "I'm sorry, Joli, but you won't be waking up from this dream."

I stopped smiling, as I could see even in her blind eyes that she wasn't lying.

I frantically pinched myself, over and over in different parts of the body, then was about to jump into the lava-

But Beleth grabbed me back, and sat me back down as I was wriggling in his arms.

The demon said, *"While I'd love nothing more than to watch you burn yourself alive and still find no relief, our Queen has this annoying policy on suffering..."*

Hanatrix waved her finger at me, and said, "Suffering is no fun! We ain't sufferin' no more! That's my motto! It's been my running slogan for years! Not like the demons have a choice but to elect me as their Queen, but it sure keeps them satisfied."

I just stared at her, and then wa wa waed my heart out, wishing I could go home...

20

"So you're saying I died of a heart problem?! I had a perfect heart, clean as all can be, too!!" I said defiantly to Hanatrix.

"Well, sometimes this happens. You actually *did* have a heart problem, but it never was detected until this fatal incident. Ever hear of spontaneous combustion? That's what this is kinda like, random, just with your heart failing!" Hanatrix said, smiling.

"...I bet someone poisoned me, or stabbed me in my sleep, and then you abducted my soul to this strange... place." I said.

Hanatrix said, "I wish that were true... It'd make it so much easier what to do with you as our prisoner! We'd get two souls for one, as soon as your murderer comes down here, as well! But nope!"

"...So... What *are* you going to do to me? I've heard such stories of Hell! Is it true Satan gets drunk and beats you as his wife?? That's what my parents always said, even though they were Wiccans and not Christians." I said, "Well, Dad was a Wiccan, Mom was a Confucist, and they always got into some crazy discussions when discussing the afterlife!"

Beleth said, *"And look, they were both wrong. Really we've got a happy go lucky Queen making us slave to build animal shelters and playgrounds..."*

"Yep!" Hanatrix said, "I think we'll start you off as... Hmm... I don't know what you should be! You actually seem to have landed here by accident. You lived a perfect life, and there's *no way* God would miss out on taking *you* to Heaven... It really baffles my bonkers..."

"Ar-Are my parents ok? I was going to see th-them soon... They must be... *heartbroken!!"* I said, and burst out crying.

Hanatrix burst out laughing, and said, "I get it! Cuz of your heart!"

I continued to cry, and Hanatrix stopped laughing.

Hanatrix frowned, and said to Beleth, "See? What am I supposed to do with a young adult like this who loves her parents, donates time at the animal shelter whenever they need her, has upstanding work ethics, was a great friend despite having no romantic interests-"

I said, "What's my sex life got to do with any of this?!"

Hanatrix said, "Nothing at all! You had none! It's been a good long while since a virgin landed in Hell with us, even though it happens."

I said, "Look here, I was just about to ask the churro guy out... when I felt like it! I was saving it for a special occasion!!"

Hanatrix politely said, "The churro guy who didn't know English, and was the age of your father's father?"

"...I thought he was cute!" I said.

Hanatrix patted my hand and said, "Let's move onto the next subject. What is it you *want* to do, in Hell? Would you like to be a demon?"

I thought about it.

I kinda did want to be a demon.

The world, God, my parents, seemed to have shunned me, let me die, and go to Hell. Would be right to turn my back on them and become an evil, malicious demon-

I sighed, and said to Hanatrix, "I'm sorry. I would desperately love to become a demon under you, but- my mom always called me her Happy Little Angel, and I don't think I could disappoint her..."

Hanatrix waved a hand incredulously at me to Beleth, and Beleth said, *"Why don't I show her the grand tour, and you can get back to work, Hana. It'll give me something to do."*

Hanatrix sighed, shook my hand, and said, "It was nice meeting you, Joli. I'll check back in on you later. Give 'em Hell!"

And poof, the blind woman popped away in smoke.

21

Beleth took me to the fire pit. He said, *"...This is a pit of fire. There are a lot of them like this one in Hell, but this is 'the' pit of fire."*

"...What makes it 'the' pit of fire?" I asked.

"It's the hot spot to go to!" Beleth said, and giggled.

"...Is Hell going to be a continuous string of bad jokes?" I said.

"...Er... Sometimes, yes. Keep this confidential between you and I, but I think Hanatrix is slipping over the years... Losing her marbles, so to say... Hell would be much better if, oh... I was ruler of Hell..." Beleth whispered.

"...Are you sowing the seeds of mutiny?" I said.

Beleth smiled, and said, *"Of course I am! It's my job to, as second in command! You see, if I spread a little discontent here and there, it keeps the rest of the demons occupied and content. If they see someone like me is working for them on the inside, they get back to work and don't complain. I'm a demon, you see, I'm supposed to be treacherous."*

"...Are you sure that's right? And you don't want to be ruler of Hell, then?" I said.

"I have something... more magnificent in mind... but just between you and me... I am ever so loyal to my Queen..." Beleth said, and beckoned me to follow him past the pit of fire.

He took me to the seventh circle, and Beleth said, *"This is where Hanatrix likes to walk her three headed guardian of Hell, Cerberus. You can see his last reign of terror in that direction, over there. I do believe he had an upset stomach that day."*

All I could see in that direction was flames and wreckage. It actually *was* different than the rest of the street, because all around us were *magnificent* houses made of brimstone, demons playing and laughing with each other here and there, asking each other howdoyoudo, and all that. I remarked to Beleth, "Wow! This isn't what I pictured of Hell at all! I expected it to be… like that direction, over there!"

"We've decided to better our lot in the afterlife, rather than squabble and bicker amongst each other under Satan, as we had for millennia before. Would you care to see the old archnemesis of creation? It's a great part of the tour." Beleth said.

"See S-Satan? Only if he doesn't beat me too hard." I said.

Beleth laughed nicely, and said, *"Hardly. He doesn't even have any appendages to do so, these days, but watch out for his appendix!"*

Beleth laughed down the street, and I followed him curiously.

We got to… a library.

Inside, there was someone reading from a burning book of a beautiful story, that was action packed, romance filled, and-

The demon reading shut the book, and said, *"And that's the story of Satan."*

The burning book said, *"Wa-Wait! I wasn't finished yet!"*

"We'll leave it on a happy ending. Book reading is at 11:00 am next week, everybody! Go out and steal from your local library, burn your best books, and then we can all discuss how we did so. Also don't forget to donate to the library, anything you can spare!"

Beleth whispered to me, *"Some of the demons get a little confused in favor of Hanatrix's policies... They don't know whether to be good or bad anymore, so just decided to do both and feel good about it."*

"Sounds reasonable. There is a great feeling in both of those acts, and I'm sure in a world where it was acceptable people would like to be both good and evil if they could." I said.

As the book reading group left, leaving the burning book on the chair, Beleth said, *"Hmph. Says the 'Happy Little Angel...' Let's go meet Satan."*

We walked up to the burning book, and I asked Beleth, "Is he invisible?? Or hiding in the shadows??"

"You're looking at him." Beleth said, waving a hand to the burning book.

The burning book sighed, as Beleth grinned, and the burning book said, *"Another 'tour,' Beleth?"*

Beleth said, *"Of course, oh grand 'master...' I love seeing you cut short, used as a paperweight, not being known where to be categorized, lost, stolen, then lost again... It brings a satisfying chill to my heart, seeing my overlord brought so low..."*

The burning book said, *"I swear you'll be the first I come for, Beleth, Demon of Music. Even before Hana... Or maybe... I'll go after this human over here. RORARARARRAAAAA!!"*

The burning book seemed to try to scare me. I just blinked at it.

"Can I read it or something?" I said.

The burning book grumbled, and whined, *"Just please, please, please no dog ears on the pages."*

I felt kind of bad for this book, whimpering at me. I reached out to touch it, and its fire tickled my hand.

I suppose even evil monsters can be pitied. Maybe that's all they should be.

I then turned to Beleth, and said, "Alright, I've seen enough of Satan. I'd love to see the park you talked about! Such new wildlife, I'm sure Hell has!"

The burning book stuttered at us as we left it on the chair, and moaned out in agony. Poor Devil.

22

I stared at the man holding a noose and reading from a book on a bench.

"You mean that's really...Judas??" I whispered to Beleth.

"Yep. He's grown a lot more relaxed over the years, after Hanatrix had a little chat with him. He decided there's so much worse suffering to be found rather than killing himself every day, so decides to take upon his eternal suffering in other ways. See, watch." Beleth said.

Judas got up from the bench and walked down the burning river of fire with his book, and then stumbled, and dropped the book into the river where it was incinerated. Judas moaned out in despair, and screamed out, *"But I'll never know the end now!! NOOOOOOO!!!!"*

He moaned in agony, on his knees, and we politely passed him down the path surrounded by evil, dead trees.

I bumped into one of the trees by accident, which said, *"Oops. My apologies. I was going to try and make you lose your way in the woods."*

The tree then shuffled back out off the path, back into the forest. I shrugged at it.

The wind screamed like people dying, but it seemed they lost their spirit for all the moaning, and took up laughing instead.

The vampire bats were so neat! I loved seeing them hang from the trees, thousands, watching me hungrily, and the roses bit me pleasantly, so friendly! Apparently animals and plants in Hell were past sinners, and they were so cute, too!

I said, "It seems Hell is... a nice place to be, nowadays. Even if all the people in it are horrible monsters, they don't seem so bad with Hanatrix as their Queen. They get along, reminisce on past horrors done, and seem generally like any normal human on Earth! Although demons are a lot more proud of killing and eating babies, then anyone I've seen on Earth ever was. I suppose they should be commended for standing tall against adversity."

Beleth said, *"Quite true. You don't know of all the souls I've spoiled and seduced in my eternity, and being able to relax after all that time is quite appeasing to me. Well. Here we are, this is the monument to the old Queen of Hell, and her husband."*

"Wow..." I said. There was a huge statue of a man kneeling before a powerful looking thin woman, offering her a ring in marriage. They were gigantic, grandiose, looked like they were really there, and so life-like that she was about to say yes to his marriage proposal.

Beleth said, *"So yes, that is the old Queen of Hell, Dina, the Conqueror of the Underworld... She vanished a good while ago, and Hanatrix was forced to assume her mother's role. Some say the old Queen is still wandering all creation as we know it, and even places beyond. The husband, Zaxazaxar, is awaiting her still in Heaven, eternally faithful."*

"So... cool! Was she magic, or something, to be able conquer *all* of Hell, all by herself?! And how come the husband didn't go with her? And if you don't mind me asking, why is Hanatrix blind?" I said.

"...That's a lot of questions I am unsuitable to answer. I can say this, however... Dina did have help, with a few generals, even though the ultimate battle was in her hands. She had me, and... those."

Beleth waved his arms at a few statues to the side. A cowman mooing, and two succubi locked in battle. I shivered when I saw them, and I said, "Looks like they're gonna jump at me at some point."

Beleth said, *"They might, but Hanatrix has seen fit that they not be released yet. Come, let us meet her eternal majesty as the eternal evening draws close..."*

I followed Beleth back down the path, looking back over my shoulder at the statues.

23

Hanatrix offered me a place to stay, in her huge castle in the underworld. I wanted to ask her all about herself and her work, but she just said, "Still? I am very tired. I just had to give two thousand new souls jobs, and we all have to work together to make sure things run smoothly in Hell… I'll see you at dinner, so allow me (yawn…) a brief nap…"

I drew in my guest room. I always loved drawing, but instead of the normal monsters and characters I drew, I decided to draw an angel instead.

I named him Tom.

He looked so nice and friendly, long hair in his eyes, and I was about to draw him some wings-

Hm. What kind of wings did Tom have? I suppose the picture was good enough as it was. Maybe he could help me figure out what wings *I* needed, one day.

I hung Tom up on the wall, and went down to dinner.

Wow! This was food like in the living world! And so much, too! I said to Hanatrix I could never eat all of this by myself!

Hanatrix said, "Call me Hana, Joli. We're friends now! And don't worry about wasting food, we always donate whatever is left to the unfortunate in Hell, and I was *going* to have them make something a little more… small, for us, but the staff were just so ecstatic to have a guest to feed…"

Beleth stood at the side, ever attentive, and said, *"It really has been so long since you've had good company, Hanatrix... I suppose you'll have to do with Joli, for now."*

Hana said, "Have you thought more about what you want to do in Hell, Joli? Or would you rather I try to appeal your case to God to have you taken up?"

"...Taken up? I don't know… I actually really like it here! You're all so friendly and charming, and I think people are missing out on not going to Hell." I said.

"Believe me, no matter how hard I try… God is always one step ahead in greatness. It's why I get all the damned souls, and he gets the ones who can actually do something to help others… I try to help my people, my demons of Hell, but angels get to do a lot of things in the living world, teach others, stop suicides, even just show kindness. You could do a lot in Heaven, Joli." Hana said.

Beleth served me some steak, macaroni, potato salad, and mashed potatoes with gravy.

I thought about Hana's offer of Heaven as I gorged myself on the food. Hana also offered me some wine, but I said, "Just water for me, please!" Hana said of course, and I got cool, chilling water, fresh from the river Styx.

I looked at my cup of water that was black.

I sipped at it carefully.

And I felt complete oblivion overtake me, in a manner of seconds, but only for a second.

"That's… some heavy water, Hana." I said.

"Oh, the food here is just something special we have stored. Something to make you feel more at home. Real hellish food is nothing like the living world, so be thankful for this meal." Hana said, smiling.

I ate the rest of my food, finished my weird water, and chatted with Hana about her day. She lived such an interesting life, and was such a powerful figure, despite being the happiest, bubbliest person I've ever met! She said we were a lot alike, and not only in bubbliness. She said I was powerful too, I just had to learn how.

I smiled at her, and Beleth escorted me back to my room.

I asked Beleth, confidentially, how he started the job as Hana's butler, anyway.

Beleth sighed angrily, and said, *"I didn't mean to! I was watching the coronation ceremony with the others, then Hana singled me out, even though blind, with a pointed finger, and said,* 'You will serve me, Beleth.' *I think she just got accustomed to me as her lifelong music teacher, as I am the Demon of Music, and wanted that familiarity as her mother disappeared..."*

I patted Beleth on the arm and said, "Well, I'm happy you took the job, Beleth. I had a great day today!"

Beleth hmphed, and said, *"I try to slink away, as I did when she singled me out, but the blind see more than they let on. Especially Hana. Well. Sweet dreams."*

Beleth then slunk away, back down the hall to Hana.

Dreams! Of course, this was just a big dream! All I had to do was fall asleep, to wake up! I excitedly snuggled into bed, with Tom the angel picture watching over me, and went back to sleep, eager to wake up from this dream...

It worked! I woke up on the couch, looking for my cat-

But everything was empty in my apartment.

The cat was gone.

I walked out of the open door, as people were moving my stuff out. I tried yelling at them to put that back, but they didn't seem to hear me.

I ran to my parent's house, past the churro guy who looked very sad, and saw one of my one friends from the animal shelter in the park! She would know what's going on!

"Shauna! Why is-" I yelled out.

She ignored me, and burst down crying, sitting on the bench.

A man noticed her, and asked if she was alright in the park.

Shauna said, "...My best friend died, and my dog died too... I... I don't know what to do, Rico..."

Rico, the man, grimaced, and offered a hug to her. She accepted, and cried on his shoulder. Rico just blinked, and looked at her sadly.

"Shauna, I'm still here for you! It's going to be ok!" I said.

She continued to cry.

I continued to run to my parents' house, scared of what was going on.

I saw them in the garden, and my mom said, "These flowers will do nice for... for Joli's funeral, I think."

I felt my heart... not beat.

My dad agreed with my mom, and they went inside.

I ran to hug them, but someone called my name from behind me.

I turned back, and woke up in... well, not fright, but surprise.

And I woke up in my bed in Hell, drenched in sweat, even though it was perfectly cool in Hanatrix's castle.

24

I had breakfast with Hanatrix. Beleth didn't seem to eat. I asked him why, and he said, *"I'm a demon, Joli. You're dead. Eating isn't necessary for us, and if I do feel like eating something I prefer a nice, fear drenched soul tortured to a crisp..."*

Hana said, "It's hard for new souls to quit the habit of eating, and in Hell people *used* to be hungry for their torment, but I allow them to eat if they feel like it, to fill the ever constant craving some demons have of the living world."

I said, "That's true. I never thought of it like that... These spicy things seem like they want to eat me, though."

Hana said, "Those are hellsbane! They grow naturally in Hell, and are quite good on toast."

I looked at the spicy berries on my plate next to my fried egg sandwich. The berries avoided my fork, but I caught one eventually and had another taste. Yep, such a weird flavor. The taste of being eaten.

Hana invited me to see what she does in Hell, that maybe that'd help me choose a demon job for myself in Hell. I accepted, and we got ready for our day!

I hummed walking with her down to her transportation in the back of the castle, and she made small talk of the weather in Hell with me, always awful but in a good way, and told me really she doesn't need transportation in Hell as its eternal ruler, really she prefers to travel by shadow, smoke, and fire.

"How does one do that again?" I asked.

"Well, you've gotta be really attuned to Hell to figure this out, and it took me a long time to learn the trick from my mother. Of course, she could also travel past the veil and through any reality she felt like, but I'm satisfied with shadow, smoke, and fire." Hana said.

We got to a large, demonic dragon, devouring a dead cow.

The dragon said, *"Good morning, Hana. Did you bring me a more wholesome snack?"*

Hana said, "Good morning, Dragon. No, this is Joli, and she's going to be traveling with us today."

Hana then jumped up onto the dragon which let her on, and I nervously tried to get onto the dragon as well. Hana helped me up behind her.

"To the Plains of Wrath, Dragon." Hana said.

Then, fwoosh, the dragon leapt into the skies of Hell as I screamed, holding onto Hana close. Hana laughed in delight.

Wow. It was so cool seeing Hell from above. All the fire, the torment and destruction, all tamed by Hana. A few demons roared and screamed up at Hana as we passed, and Hana waved hello to them.

Then we heard the sounds of battle, and landed in the Plains of Wrath.

We looked on at the eternal war from a hilltop, and Hana said, "You could be a demon of battle, Joli. Eternal wrath. Some demons still have a lot of anger, and continue to wage their wars throughout the underworld, for all time. It keeps them occupied."

Hana's dragon then flew over the field, and a demon in a trench shouted, *"The Queen approaches! Cease fire!"*

And lo and behold, the demons of wrath had peace, kneeling before their Queen dismounting in the center of the carnage. I jumped off the dragon beside her, landing on my face in some bloody mud.

Demons from the opposing sides ran up to Hana, and Hana asked, "What's the fight about this time? And the casualties?"

A demon soldier saluted, and said, *"We've slaughtered at least five thousand souls in battle, dear Queen, all for your majesty."*

A demon from the other side said, *"Well we've poisoned their supplies, and have taken at least half of that number prisoner for torture and interrogation, dear Queen, all for your majesty."*

I asked Hana, "...What happens to demons when they die?"

"Hm? Oh, watch this." Hana said.

Hana opened her hand to one of the demons, and the demon immediately gave her a pistol.

I started to protest, no one needed to die! But Hana shot one of the soldiers in the head, and he fell to the ground, bleeding out.

The other soldier cheered, and said, *"We have victory! Celebrate, everyone, for the Queen has delivered the final blow! Christmas is coming, sweethearts!"*

And all the demons cheered, and packed up from their war, going home.

I looked at the dead demon, feeling kind of sad for him, but pretty soon Hana helped him back up, and the demon congratulated Hana on a fine shot.

Hana gave him back his pistol, and said to me, "Well, he *was* already dead. Does this kind of job suit you?"

I said, "...No, not really. I don't think I could ever cause someone suffering based on my wrath."

Hana shrugged, and said to the soldier, "You've done a fine job, soldier. Now have peace, until you find something else to quarrel about."

The soldier saluted, tears in his eyes, and said, *"Thank you, my Queen."*

He then ran off with the others, and we got back on the dragon to go to the House of Lust.

25

Hana winked at me, and said, "Never too late to lose it! I think you'll like being a succubus."

I looked at her nervously, and thought of all the people I wish I had the courage to start a relationship with in the living world... We flew over the city, and soon landed before a huge mansion.

We walked through the doors as the dragon sat outside. It was dark, shadowy... and very bright red, in the House of Lust.

A succubus came to us, and said, *"Oooh... Hana, you're looking marvelous today. Can I get you something? Something... hot... You warm me up, whenever I see you again, dear!"*

Hana smiled, and said, "I'd love a day to relax with you, Selma, but I actually was wondering if you could teach my protege, Joli here, what you gals and guys do."

The succubus swished her tail back and forth, and said, *"Oooh... Fresh meat. Should I give her the whole experience, or just an onlooker's perspective?"*

Hana looked at me, kinda at me but not directly, and I nervously said, "J-Just an onlooker's perspective, will be fine, thanks."

The succubus purred, and said, *"Suit yourself. We're always eager for some new plaything, in the House of Lust. Come, let me see if I can't change your mind, with a few of the new incubi..."*

I blushed, as we got to a room with a few naked male demons, incubi, who were smiling and winking at me.

Hana felt a few of the demons, cuz she was blind, touching their faces and bodies here and there, and she said, "Mmm... I like this one, this one with the prominent jaw... You guys get better and better feeling every time I come here! Would you care to have a go with any of these young studs, Joli?"

I felt like my face was filled to the brim with red, and couldn't even get a word out.

The succubus said, *"...Oh. I think I see the problem. Your friend, Hana, seems to be a little shy."*

Hana said, "Hm? Oh! Oh... I'm sorry, Joli. We see lust as a good thing down in Hell, and not something to be ashamed of. I'm going to discuss with Selma about her work, and howbout you get to know some of these lads? You'll see they're more than the lust they portray."

The succubus, Selma, said, *"Take five, everyone! Get to know the new girl when you can."*

The incubi breathed out a sigh of relief, and a few of them started playing cards in a corner. Selma and Hana went to a room in the back.

I nervously tried to approach one of the incubi smiling sexily at me, and he patted a seat beside him, a low pillow. I nervously sat next to him, and said, "S-So you like it? Having a lot of sex?'

He shrugged, and said, *"It's what I died from. STDs and all that. Can be a painful way to go, when you die because you can't... fulfill your bodily urges safely. It was all fun and games until the docs came out..."*

I said, "So... Do you miss it? Being in the living world?"

"Actually... No. I did some very disturbing and fucked up things for sex, and when they asked me if I was sorry for it, even as I lay dead, I said no. I enjoyed my time in life, and then I learned that there's a free opening in Hell for incubi, and I just couldn't resist." the incubi said.

"Do you... Do you wish you could've had that relationship with someone, even if that person was as fucked up and disturbing as you? Not that you're disturbing. I actually feel strangely comfortable with you." I said.

He smiled charmingly to me, and said, *"That's the number one opening to a woman's... y'know. Make them feel comfortable. I do sometimes wish I could've met an alike soul, but that's the thing. Here in Hell there are so many just like me, and having that exclusive companionship, with everyone, really makes me feel at home."*

I smiled, blushed, and said if he ever decides to get bored of fucking around, I'd be around to fuck. I was in Hell. I had nothing to lose at this point.

"Dominus." he said, offering a hand to shake.

"Joli. The pleasure is mine." I said, shaking his hand.

The incubus and I were soon kissing sweetly, when Hana came back out. Hana said, "C'mon, Joli... Selma and I... Mmm... Just, c'mon, Joli. We've gotta go."

Selma teased Hana, saying, *"You're more shy than your protege! Later, dearie! I'll always be... hot, for you, my Queen..."*

I waved the incubus, Dominus, goodbye, and followed Hana back to the dragon. Hana looked as red as a rose, and her clothes were all ruffled. I wondered if...

She said, "So. Is the job of a lustful succubus appealing to you?" as we got on the dragon.

"I don't know. I think it's something I was missing, but I really prefer a one on one relationship, rather than having sex with more than I can count." I said.

Hana shrugged, and said, "Suit yourself. To the Bazaar of Greed! Let's go shopping!"

26

The dragon lumbered down the street to the Bazaar of Greed, where there were merchants of all types selling… everything! One was trying to barter his soul for a brand new robe, sexual acts were currency, and the *gold...* Some of the people were glittering with wealth that bedazzled the eyes.

Hana said to me, "I made the wealth of Hell for all. There are actually a few dense caches of Hellish minerals here, and I made sure it wasn't exclusively for the upper class, to toy with the lower demons."

A merchant was selling notes of his song, and was being thrown gold pieces for each note. The music sounded beautiful and mysterious, as the clink of gold continued the percussion.

Hana stopped at a food merchant, something for her staff to like, and haggled the demon to death. She told me to go look around, and that she would be here for a while.

I saw a familiar demon walk into a shop down a dark alley, and I decided to follow him.

I walked through the abyssal darkness, shadows whispering to me as I passed, and opened the door which the little bell tinkled me greetings.

There I saw Beleth say to the shopkeeper, *"So is it ready yet?"*

The shopkeeper said, *"Let me check the back- Oh! Welcome to Souls and Shambles, my shop, dear lady... My... That's some interesting looking human skin you have, you wouldn't be in the market to sell it would you?"*

I shook my head, and Beleth jumped as he saw me. I asked him, "Whatcha doin' here? Getting a gift for Hana?"

Beleth blinked, and said, *"Of... course. This is hardly a place for a prim and proper lass like yourself, now... Why don't you check out the sweets and candy vendors?"*

I said, "Nah. I never ate candy, to keep healthy. What do you sell, mister?"

The shopkeeper demon grinned, and said, *"Souls... and the shambles of them. Here you can trade your very soul for marvelous trinkets, or credit with any demon in the lowest abyss... The shambles are the leftovers, little scraps of emotion and feeling, that one wants to get rid of for pocket change."*

Beleth said, *"It's quite a good deal. I pick up- shambles of music from Heaven when I can."*

I wowed, and said, "You can get shambles of Heaven here? That is a good deal! What if- What if I want to forget about… people… from the living world? I'd be able to sell them here, right?"

The shopkeeper bowed, and said, *"You'd be paid most well. You seem like your shambles are still intact, and ripe for plucking, dear lady..."*

Beleth said, *"I'll... just come back another day, before-"*

Hana burst into the shop, looking pissed.

She said, *"Beleth! What* have I *told* you about coming here?! And Joli, this is *not* the place for you."

Beleth stuttered, *"But I get the shambles straight from a connect in Heaven! Y'know, Ronnie? He sometimes just wants some peace and quiet from the music in his head after a long day, and sells them to me!!"*

I stuttered, "And I don't *want* to remember my time in the living world!! I just- I just want to forget about it..."

Hana looked at me, sorta directly, with a sympathetic look on her face. She said, "Joli. Those memories are very precious, and should never be given away lightly."

The shopkeeper said, *"And very precious they are! Ok, I'll throw in a brand new indentured servant for her shambles-"*

Even though blind, Hana stared daggers into the shopkeeper, and the shopkeeper shut up.

She said, "We'll take the servant, and also Beleth's 'shambles.' I'll show you both that you're being ripped off. Think of this as a gift to the Queen, shopkeep. A gift of less torture and suffering on your end."

The shopkeeper gulped, and went to the back, where he came back with a jar of something swirling around in it, and... a young human boy.

27

We took the young boy and the shambles back to the castle, and Hana told Beleth and I to take a seat. She stroked the young boy's face who was standing at the ready for her, who had a listless look in his eyes. Hana said, "For the first thing, let me show you these 'shambles' are really a gift from Ronnie himself, hand crafted for you, Beleth. I think he still thanks you for some things in his past era of King of Hell, and I think you should cut him loose, Beleth."

Beleth said, *"Oh, hogwash. I'm sure I must be getting delectable pieces of soul from Heaven herself-"*

Hana opened the jar with the swirling thing in it, and beautiful, enchanting music came out, sung by a man with a powerful voice.

Beleth sighed in happiness as he heard that, and we listened to the music which changed into heavy metal after a second.

Hana said, as the music still played, "This is a very precious thing. You've been given a gift of being able to brush up against this angel, and know this... that time has ended."

Beleth nodded sadly, and just... listened to the music.

Hana said, "And this boy... This is a soul that belongs in Heaven."

I gasped, and a bright light appeared in Hana's hand. She touched the boy's forehead, and he gasped, then looked very frightened. He said, "Wh-Where am I?? What's going on?"

Hana held his hand gently, and said, "You're going home, dear. I just need to contact an angel of death."

We heard slamming on the castle door, and Hana waved her hand and allowed the slammer entry.

A short angel came in, looking *furious.* He said, "Hana. I've been looking for *ages* for this soul. I only felt his soul come back together from pieces just now. *What* have you been doing to him?!"

Hana said, "Max. I think you've been slipping at your job lately. I don't know how this soul got to Hell, but it may have something to do with Joli being here too. Please, take him off my hands, and I will make the proper inspections *immediately.*"

Max opened his arms for the young boy, crying as he was, and the young boy ran to Max's hug.

Max whispered, "It'll be ok now, Norman. It'll be ok." Max looked at Hana, still in his hug, and said, "What about her?" talking about me.

Hana said, "She's in safe hands, and doesn't know specifically where she wants to go as of yet. I'll be watching her closely."

Max nodded, and said, "I wish you left all of Hell to itself, and just came to Heaven, Hana... but I see this place needs you. Well. I'll see you around."

Max then took the crying boy out the doors, and the doors shut behind him.

The shambles ended their music, and Beleth woke up from his trance. He said, *"I suppose all music must hit the final bar, at some point."*

28

"I've been meaning to tell you that the Palace of Pride and Enclave of Envy have been doing some reasonably shady things..." Beleth said.

"*What* sort of shady things?" Hana said.

Beleth said, *"Well... They're always trying to overthrow you, and you know that already, but they mentioned something to me about fresh souls. Hard to remember, now that I think back on it. Pride just goes to your head, you know? But if anyone has the motives and means to steal clean human souls, it's those two 'organizations.'"*

Hana sighed, and said, "Must I go all wrath and brimstone already? I wanted to show Joli here the *pleasant* parts of Hell, and not the dull power plays for meager superiority. Oh well... I suppose you *must* see me air my dirty laundry... Come, Joli. Hold my hands. We will be traveling to the Enclave of Envy through shadow. Beleth? Hold down the fort, and make inspections for any other pure souls in Hell."

Beleth bowed to Hana, and I held Hana's hands.

I immediately felt... so dark, and cold, and... shadowy...

Like... my world... was only black...

Like... the cold abyss... was really... everywhere...

I just... continued... to follow Hana... this bright... light... in the... darkness...

I gasped in front of a dark blackness, only shadows ahead, and I looked down at my body and I wasn't darkness anymore.

Hana said, "No good for you to go in as a shadow at this point… You'd lose your way fast. They've seemed to have darkened the Enclave, in wait for me… Ha! As if that could stop the Queen. My world is *always* shadow… Just hold onto my hand, Joli, and we'll get through Envy."

Hana led me through the darkness with her blind eyes and other senses, and I just clung onto her warm, soft hand close.

We want your light.

Something whispered to me.

We want your life.

Something touched my shoulder.

We want your soul.

And then Hana lit fire all around her, and I saw millions of demons appear from the shadows, blinded by Hana's light.

"Yet you will have none." Hana boomed.

One of the demons groveled before Hanatrix, and said, *"Give us just a taste... Give us only a memory... We need it... Please, oh damned Queen... Oh please..."*

Hanatrix boomed, *"Where have you been taking the pure souls?"*

The demon begged, *"We didn't know, oh sovereign... We didn't know... We still don't... We desperately need them, but the Palace-"*

Hanatrix boomed, *"Where?"*

The demon muttered, *"They are a feast of delight... that none of us can eat... Please, a touch, oh Queen... A touch of delight..."*

The demon raised a hand to touch Hanatrix, and Hana held his hand gently.

The demon looked like he wanted to clutch onto more, to grab and grab at Hana, but… he let his arm fall to his side, and bowed low before the Queen.

Hana said, "Come, hold my hand, Joli. We will be traveling through smoke and fire."

I held Hana's hand, and we ignited into flame, leaving the Enclave of Envy back to its grasping shadows.

29

It hurt.

It was hot.

It was fire.

And I was fire.

And then the smoke.

We traveled like a supernova through Hell, faster than even lightning, in intense, burning heat.

And like a crack of a spark, we landed before the Palace of Pride, which seemed to be holding a masquerade ball.

Hana accepted masks and makeshift horns from Beleth, who seemed to have been waiting for us. Beleth said, *"They've been trying to get you to a party of theirs for ages now. Shame you have to accept on such a dirty business... Soul thievery, what a pity..."*

Hana put on her black and white masquerade mask, with a long nose at the tip, with the demon horns on her head, and I got a golden mask with big cheeks plus my own demon horns. Beleth put on a cat mask.

We walked through the crowds of demons, as they were all talking jubilantly and laughing in delight for the Palace of Pride's masquerade ball. I heard one say that the masks come off at midnight.

I sampled the punch, as Beleth and Hana danced a ballroom dance. She danced so delicately, and seemed to know all the moves despite being blind as a bat. I wowed at them. Maybe Beleth was just a good partner for Hana, and helped her dance correctly, but I don't think so. I think Hana could dance any demon here's socks off. The punch tasted, in a strange way… filthy. Nothing like Hana's delectable food, more like it wanted to show itself off as superior, but strangely… came up wanting.

I waited for midnight, and a demon asked me to dance.

I accepted in surprise, and he took me by the waist and kissed me softly. I then recognized this demon… Dominus!

"Oh! Pleasure to meet you again, my pleasurable demon! What are you doing in a place like *this??"* I asked.

Dominus said, through his mask of a human face, *"It's where I can be myself. Most don't look favorably on eternal lust, even in Hell, until they... wear a mask. Sex is so delicate, don't you agree? It notably shrivels with the lights on."*

I agreed, as I loved to feel this demon's body in my arms, dancing with me so gently, dancing to exquisite, strangely tasteless, music in this masquerade ball, concealed and unannounced.

He had the gall to ask if I would like to have a quickie on the terrace with him.

I blushed, and said, "That's… kinda something I always wished I could do! But midnight is approaching, and I do wish to see what Hana will do…"

Dominus shrugged, and said, *"With your fine features, I'd imagine a quickie is preferable after the masquerade has fallen. Let's wait and see what the Queen will do."*

I blushed, which thankfully Dominus couldn't see under my mask, and we held hands waiting for midnight to approach.

Hana made the move before midnight, a minute before.

The demons were about to announce some special "guests," but Hana tore off her mask and said, *"And yet you shall only meet my wrath."*

The demons gasped before the Queen, and the head demon, the Prince of Pride as he was called, said, *"We mean no hostility, oh great Queen!! Come, see before us our bountiful gifts for you-"*

Hana said, "I care not for these gifts, and they will be taken straight back to their home immediately. I only desire one thing, suitable for one as prideful as you… I desire your torture. Come, kneel before your Queen, and learn your lesson."

Hana gave Beleth a bright light, and he went to the back to free the pure souls. The pure souls filed out after Beleth, in fear of all the demons. Beleth said, *"These were the special meal to a hearty full course of soul… Delicious as they might be, they do not belong in our domain."*

Hana then took out a knife, as the guilty demon knelt before her.

She said to me, "I was top in my class of disembowlement and torture. I'd step out for a moment, unless you *really* want to see what it means to be a demon of pride, Joli. It is to have your pride… cut… low."

I walked out with Dominus, as the Prince of Pride began to scream under Hana's blade.

I had sex with an incubus, on the terrace, looking out across all of Hell… Gosh… What a sight… What a *feeling…*

Is it really losing your virginity after you're dead? Oh well, it was a great time! Dominus was so gentle… caring… pleasurable… I never thought a demon of *lust* could be all those things!

Dominus said, when we were kissing after on the terrace, *"See me more later, if you'd like to know how sex can also not be those things… But take care, Joli. I love our special romance. It brings a warm chill to my sexual organ, whenever I think on it."*

I slapped his butt as he walked away, and smiled saying, "Come... and get some whenever you like, Dominus! I'd love to learn more how you got the name!"

Dominus winked at me without his mask, and sauntered down the road of Hell, his shirt over his shoulder as he whistled in content.

30

Hana made some coffee for Beleth and I back at the castle, and we discussed how these souls got to Hell in the first place. They were taken in droves by angels back to Heaven.

Hana said, "It seems these souls never got to Heaven, but were meant to be there. They just somehow... got lost, after their death. The demons of envy and pride aren't really sure how they did, same as us, actually, but I'm certain to find out soon..."

Beleth said, *"Those demons really just wanted to take a firmer stance against you. You know the demons of envy always want what they can't have, and the demons of pride think they have it."*

"Quite true, Beleth. Say, Joli, did you have any sort of premonition or anything of the sorts before you died?" Hana said.

"...Well... I always did dream of dying, even as a kid, and I learned to like them, in a weird way. Nothing of the sort before my death, though. I thought I was just taking a nap!" I said.

Hana said, "Were these souls predestined to death before life? No, that's how life works already... I'm going to pray, and see if God can give me any guidance."

I said, "You *pray??* I thought the Queen of Hell didn't like praying."

Hanatrix smiled sort of at me, and said, "A common misconception! I found God too, strangely, I just also, y'know, am in eternal Hell. I'll pray with you guys, would you care to join me?"

Beleth said, *"...I think I'm fine, thanks. You do you."*

I said, "Sure! I love other religions, they can all be seen in such a unique way!"

I held hands with Hana, and she prayed.

I felt... I don't know. I think I felt good, even though I was in Hell. Like God was looking after me still. I felt really good, but it was hard to explain how.

Then, crack, an angel appeared behind Hana. I gasped, as the man looked sort of like Hana, black hair, and had an extra incisor in his smile.

Hana said, "Wh-Who's there?? Don't play any pranks, God. I'm not up to it at the moment."

The man said, "Hana, I would never deceive you. I'm so happy to see you again."

Hana gasped in surprise, and said, "D-Dad?? Please, come to me. I can't see you."

The man instantly rushed to Hana, and they hugged.

They were crying soon, as Hana felt his face.

She cried on his shoulder, in his embrace, and she said, "I'm *so* happy to feel you again, Dad... I-I-I never thought- I thought I'd never see- Never hug you again."

The man continued to cry, and said, "I was always here for you, Hana. Since when you first were born, I will always look after you. Say, where's Cerberus, anyway? I'd like to meet that snarling monstrosity again, too."

Hana laughed, and said, "He's been guarding the exit to Hell, since we really can't have another thing like the Devil's Daughter escaping, now can we? That was a whole bunch of weirdness, that frankly the world was unaccustomed to."

The man laughed, and said, "I'd offer to take you away from here immediately, but I see you've found your purpose. I am so proud of you, Hana."

Hana laughed while crying, and said, "These are my friends. You remember Beleth, right? He's my butler now. And this is Joli, a very special soul indeed."

The man nodded to Beleth, which Beleth nodded back lounging on his chair, and the man shook my hand and said, "I'm Zaxazaxar. Call me Zax."

I was all watered up too from this reunion, and I shook his hand, saying, "Lafaya Joliet Bonaparte, but call me Joli."

31

I let Hana and her dad reconnect, as they seemed to have a lot to talk about, the least not being the missing souls of Heaven, and I went to the kitchen staff to meet them.

I saw a drunk man gulping down vodka.

I saw a wiry woman splashing salt on everything.

And I saw a hunchback with one bulbous eye and one normal one, stirring stew.

They were all singing together, hey, hey, hey, as they cooked together.

The drunk man said, *"Hey... Now! We've gooooot a visitor!"*

The wiry woman said, *"Does she need any salt?? I've got so much salt thanks to Hana's deal with that merchant!! You need some salt?!"*

The hunchback mumbled quietly, and nodded at me.

I said hi to everyone! I introduced myself as Joli, and they all cheered in glee!

The drunk man said, *"Weeeeee (hiccup) neeeeed someone to cook for. Hana... really knows her food! Taught us everything she knows, and alwwaaaays lets us surprise her with something neeeeeeeeeeeeeeeeeeeeeeeeeeeeeeeeeeeeeeeeeeeeeeeeeeeeew."*

I paused after his long new, and the wiry woman said, *"You need paprika flakes?! I know you need some paprika flakes!? Let me splash a bit here!!"*

The wiry woman then splashed paprika flakes on the dish, and the hunchback man mumbled and nodded.

I sang with them for a bit, singing an old song I grew up with.

"Hey now, the rock's down low!" I sang.

"Hey now, the stone don't throw!" they sang.

"Hey now, the river is fine!"

"Hey now, the trees are pine!"

"Hey, hey, now, Crix is the town!"

"Hey, hey, now, don't have a frown!"

"Because in Crix town, the frown's upside down!"

They laughed with me, and I was surprised they knew the song my parents' sang to me as a child.

I waved them goodbye, and went to have one last talk with (my boyfriend?) Dominus.

He waited for me on the steps of the castle, smoking a cigarette.

He held my hand as I sat with him.

He said, *"I don't want to alarm you, but I had sex with at least five other people after we did it."*

I shrugged, and snuggled up with him. I said, "As long as you're true to yourself, that's ok with me..."

He snuggled with me. We just sat looking out on Hell. It seemed there was a riot going on, nothing to worry about Dominus assured, just the locals having fun.

I said to him, "Would you love me, if you could?"

He said, *"...What makes you think I can't love you?"*

I said, "Oh, I don't know. Something with the having sex with everybody thing. Doesn't that make you, like, worn out from love, or something?"

He said, *"...I never thought of it like that. Would you like it if I... loved you?"*

"I'd like that very much, Dominus." I said, looking deep into his eyes.

He looked back, but gulped, and quickly looked away.

Dominus said, *"...I... I think I have to do some soul searching, figure some things out... I honestly thought you were just an easy lay with light baggage, but... I never knew there could be such an opportunity tied in with the deal. Please. Allow me to- To find my soul."*

I asked him, "Did you lose it, or something?"

He said, *"...It's probably spread halfway through Hell, the way I've sold it. I... I need to go..."*

I held his hand before he could leave, and said, "Can I help you find your soul?"

Dominus gulped as he looked at me... but nodded.

He ran to me, kissed me as I kissed him back, then tipped his cap at me, and left, running down the road to find his soul. I waved to him, and he turned while running to wave back.

The kitchen staff served me a snack, and it was so salty and paprikaey! But it really hit the spot!

I then went to bed, and had dreams of coming back to life again. Strange, how now that I was dead my dreams were reversed.

32

Hana gave me a Hellphone if I needed to contact her, and was going to spend the day reconnecting with her dad after he dropped by to visit. I had never seen her so happy, than holding her dad's hand.

I met Dominus in the castle, and he was intent on having lustful relations as I was getting ready in the shower, but I said, "I think we should find the first piece of your soul, first, don't you? I think you'll see you were missing something important in sex, and it could be your soul."

He still bit his lip, watching me bathe, and I had to draw the curtain with a smile so he wasn't tempted too hard.

Dominus and I, after Dominus splashed his face with cold water and I had gotten dressed, planned out the first place his first half of soul might be.

Dominus said, *"Well, I sold it to Belphegor, the Guardian of Sloth, awhile back so I wouldn't have to do any real work besides selling my body, so I think he's still got my half of soul in that empty bottle of booze. You know sloth guardians... They don't do anything with something once they have it..."*

"Great! Hana's taking her dad to see Cerberus on the dragon, so I guess... hmm... We can travel by shadow? I think... I know how to do that, thanks to Hana!" I said.

Dominus said, *"That's a very dangerous route to go. But I trust you. What else have I got to lose?"*

I nodded, and held his hand, then... I... went... into... the... realm of shadow...

I saw... Dominus... with me... and I... could not... tell his form from... the rest... of the darkness...

We... *We...* were darkness... unholy shadow...

A shadow grabbed my hand... Was that... Dominus?

I gasped in front of a lamp on the street in the morning of Hell, Dominus holding my hand.

He scowled at me, and said, *"Don't lose yourself in shadow, Joli."*

I nodded, feeling so cold. I asked Dominus for a hug, and he hugged me, pressing his warm, demonic body to me close.

We walked to a foreman's office, where apparently the workers here were working on a road for at least two thousand years, never finished "yet," thanks to the Guardian of Sloth, Belphegor. The workers lazed around and smoked cigarettes, not really doing any work.

We knocked on the door, and it was silent.

Dominus slammed it open, as I protested that wasn't polite, but Dominus looked in, and said Belphegor wasn't in.

Hmm... Where would a demon of sloth be if he was supposed to be working? Oh! I know.

I went to the port o potty, and knocked on it, saying we'd like to see the Guardian of Sloth, Belphegor.

A demon moaned from inside, and said, *"Gimme a minute, ok? Can't you see I'm busy?"*

Dominus and I waited for a minute, then for ten minutes, then for half an hour, and I knocked again, impatient.

The demon moaned again, and said, *"Look, I've got a busy day here! My bowels are exploding!"*

Dominus slammed open the door, and we saw a skinny, old demon reading from a nudey magazine on the toilet.

He groaned, and said, *"What now? I'm working hard, been at this road for two thousand years, I deserve a bit of a break."*

Dominus growled at him, but I said, "We want Dominus's piece of soul back, please. We could work something out?"

The demon groaned at the word "work," and I realized my faux paus.

I said, "Er… We would rather like to give you a break, but…"

Belphegor grumbled, and said, *"Who says I need you to take a break? Dominus sold his piece of soul to me, fair and square. What work have you done to deserve it, Dominus?"*

Dominus stuttered, and said, *"Truthfully, none. But Joli says I could have it back, if I wanted, and that I could be happy with it. I want that chance to have my soul back."*

I said, "How about this. We get the Queen of Hell to get you new jobs!"

Belphegor grumbled, and said, *"Then I'd have to work on ANOTHER road... Work, work, work... That's all I'm good for..."*

I hmmed at this, and said, "Well, what if we worked on this road together? I'm sure we could get the road done in no time! I know all sorts of people who'd help, let me just make a call…"

Belphegor gasped, and said, *"You wouldn't dare. This is an easy paycheck, and I'm not losing it to a bunch of upstart demons who think they know what a soul is worth. You want to know what your soul is worth, Dominus? It's worth getting you both to leave me alone. Go on, shoo."*

Belphegor then threw the soul bottle of booze at me which I caught, and slammed the port o potty door shut. I opened the soul bottle, and dripped it out onto my hand. It was viscous, but pure.

I immediately saw all the horrible, perverted things Dominus had done for work, sometimes at work, in his time alive. I shrugged at it. At least he made work exciting, for her, her, her, him, him, her, and it.

I placed the bit of soul on Dominus's forehead, and it absorbed into him.

He gasped, and said, *"Wow. I feel so energetic! Let's go and... hmm... Let's go somewhere private, where we can be alone..."*

I smiled, and he led me down the road to an abandoned alley of Hell.

33

Woah! What a... What a damn good bit of fucking! He instantly felt ten times more spritely, energetic, and just, whoosh! We both felt amazing, after that brief segment of intercourse in the alley!

We got dressed, still panting after orgasm, and walked back out of the alley to the Gluttony Grill. Dominus said he sold the other piece of his soul there, so that he would never have to focus on his desire for life, and eternally focus on sex.

"Isn't sex just part of life, though?" I asked, as we ambled down the street.

"Well, yes, but more for some than others. I wanted to get rid of the parts of my life that I needed to live, like eating, drinking, sleeping, all that. No one can do that better than a demon of gluttony, that's for sure. I've never felt hungry ever, after I got rid of that half of soul." Dominus said.

I said, "Eating and drinking feel so good, though! Even if you can't do it always!"

"Trust me, these guys do it always... Be ready to be disgusted." Dominus said.

We got to a nice restaurant, with- oh. Really fat demons! They were gorging themselves on the food, taking up the size of two tables with their gut alone!

I asked a server, who was strangely really thin, if we could see the owner to get back Dominus's soul.

The server smiled wickedly, and said, *"That'd be me, sweet. I am the established owner of the Gluttony Grill, and I can make any pleasure of yours, regarding gluttony, completely possible..."*

I looked back at Dominus, and I'm sure if he was a cat, he'd be all puffed up and bristled in anger.

Dominus said, *"Give me my soul, Beelzebub."*

"I'm the bub with the sub! That's my advert. Quite a good sub, we make, care to try one? I only talk business at lunch." Beelzebub said.

Dominus looked like he wanted to decline, but I decided to play this demon's game, and accepted a nice meal, only something small. I assured him I was watching my weight.

Beelzebub just said, *"Of course. Quite a good habit, get whatever you like, on the house for such charming guests... I'll meet you over there, the table by the window."*

I shrugged, and Dominus and I went to get food from the buffet. Dominus said he wasn't hungry, never has been, and went to sit with Beelzebub, waiting for me.

I got a little bit... then I just piled my plate with food... It all looked so good... Oh wait, I didn't want that, I wanted that... Oh, I'll just get both... I couldn't resist taking a bite of a chicken wing, just a taste... I was soon gobbling down the wing, it was so good... And was this wine? Ohmygosh, I never had something so good in all my life! And so heady, too! Mmm... Pigs in a blanket... Yum, yum, yum! I nudged a demon beside me away from them! They were mine! I snarfed down those delicious little pigs, and the demon was soon fighting me for them... I screamed and shouted at him, as I continued to eat... Oh... The build your own sub station… I piled the pigs in a blanket on some bread, and ate my pigs in a blanket sub…

I looked at Dominus, who was arguing with Beelzebub. Wasn't I doing something? Maybe I should drink more wine to remember…

I got a call from my Hellphone. What was that noise? I carefully answered, wiping the grease off my face. Hana said, "How are you doing, Joli? We have dinner at 6:00, so don't be late! My dad and I have been having such a great time!! It's so nice I can show at least one of my parents my work."

I said, "Dinner?" and then I felt oh so full.

My stomach grumbled, and I started throwing up all over the food, which the other demons ignored and ate from anyway.

I think… that completely turned off my appetite. I dropped my plate to the floor and went to Dominus and Beelzebub.

Beelzebub just laughed and laughed at me, as Dominus scowled at him. Beelzebub said, *"Here... Here! Take it! Such a good soul, falling so low for her appetite! And she said she was 'watching her weight!' Go on, get the Hell out of my restaurant, and never come back. Here's your pitiful excuse of a soul, Dominus. It tastes kinda funny, if you ask me, but not in a ha ha way."*

Beelzebub handed Dominus a glass salt shaker, and Dominus pocketed it as we left. I felt sick to my stomach.

34

Dominus said, *"So... they've been eating my soul... I feel like I should just throw it in the garbage, it's so worthless..."*

I said, as I continued to wipe my face off on my sleeve, "No! I think it's something marvelous! Here. Let me apply it to you, and you'll see you're not so bad!"

He gave me the salt shaker, and I unscrewed the lid and poured the soul salt onto my hand. I immediately saw him eating and drinking, always drunk practically, taking ladies and men to back rooms, and not even remembering the time... Doing so much drugs, and eating whatever his current relationship would give him... I thought hey, if anyone could get out of a tough spot, it'd be Dominus. It was resourceful, y'know?

I applied the salt soul to his forehead, and immediately his stomach grumbled.

I smiled, and said, "Let's go to Hana's castle, and feed you something good."

He nodded immediately, and we traveled by fire and smoke to the castle.

Hot.

Hurt.

Bad.

Ouch.

And that is all.

Then we were in front of Hana's castle.

At the castle, I declined most of the food, and just picked at a light salad. Dominus chowed down like nothing else, crying in delight that he's never had something so good in all his life and afterlife.

Hana smiled towards him, and her dad pet Cerberus, the giant three headed guardian of Hell dog. Cerberus and him seemed to have a history, and got along better because of it. Beleth continued to stand ever attent, looking kind of bored.

I took Dominus to my room with me, and I needed to show him the last part of soul he was missing... the lust part. He said, *"But don't I have that part the most?"*

"I think you've been missing something else, like I have. You've been missing love." I said.

Dominus looked at me kind of embarrassed, and sighed. He walked out to the balcony and had a cigarette, and I followed him.

We sat on the patio, looking on at Hell, and he said, *"I thought I loved someone once. It turned out to only be obsession... and lust. Love never lasts, is what I'm told, but lust always remains."*

"I think there's all sorts of love. The angel of love in my dreams always tells me so, anyway!" I said.

Dominus looked at me, and said, *"What does she say about me?"*

I said, "Well, she said you're an odd case, being damned eternal, but that doesn't always have to be. She said, give him a breather. A good break, and that I'll see by giving you a break, I'll get a break, and love will come so much easier. She seemed kind of flustered, that Nevaeh, about our relationship, though... She just said to take it slow, and then-"

Dominus kissed me.

I kissed him back.

I said, "-then we can take it fast."

We got undressed, and went to bed.

And after, I stroked his human features, so remarkable, and nothing demonic about them. He was just like me.

35

In the morning, Dominus was flexing in the mirror, combing his hair with the comb, and said, "Holy fucking goddamnit! I thought I looked hot as an incubus! THIS- This is just too good to keep to myself. You've gotta be a soul binder, or something, Joli!"

"What's that again?" I said, yawning in bed.

"I don't think Hell's ever had one besides briefly, and those are only legend! It's someone who brings souls back together from their pieces! You could be helping all sorts of demons become... just like me and you!! And Hana! Maybe she could help you? I always did wonder why our Queen had nothing demonic about her..."

I jumped out of bed, got dressed, and said, "That's a good idea!! I can't wait to start my new job as a soul binder! Thank you so much, Dominus!!"

He gently held my hands, and said, "I will always be thanking you, Joli, no matter what. I'll keep this marvelous gift you've given me, my soul, close."

He then whooped down the castle halls, shirtless, exclaiming to every demon who passed, "Joli's a soul binder!! Go to her to get your soul back!! GOOD MORNING, EVERYBODY!!"

Well, at least I had good advertisement, in my new job.

I sat with Dominus and Hana, as her dad went back to work in Heaven, (I think he was an artist angel, or something? Hana said he likes to switch jobs a lot.) and we talked at breakfast.

Dominus said, in between gulps of his food, "So… Yeah! Joli is- Oh my god this is so good… A soul binder!! You gotta help her out, oh glorious Queen!"

Hana looked kinda directly at me, and said, "Hm? Really… Well, I always thought one of those could be handy. I assumed no one wanted their souls back in Hell!"

Dominus shook his head, drank at his juice, and said, "Nuh uh. I didn't want my soul at first… But I feel so good with it… being me! It's a strange feeling."

One of the servants, a demon, came up to me and meekly said, *"Can you please... Give me back my soul? I don't think it's worth much... I did horrible things, and never asked for forgiveness... But I'd- I'd just like the chance to."*

I held her hand, looked into her hollow eyes, and said I knew where to start.

I yelled at Beleth to give her back her piece of soul, and Beleth jumped. He said, *"I... er, I've got quite a... healthy, soul collection stored up... Does this mean I have to get rid of them, Hana?"*

Hana said, "If that's what Joli says! I name you an official soul binder, Joli! You have complete authority in all manners of the soul, and only answer to me if I ask. Have fun!"

Hana sipped at her water of oblivion, and Beleth sighed and gave the servant back her piece of soul. Dominus grinned and winked at me. I felt so happy!

It was a loooong day trying to get everyone their pieces of souls back, and I fell asleep after I made a good dent of progress, next to Dominus, with a smile on my face.

36

I watched my funeral in the dream. It was nice, but it seemed like a lot of people didn't know what to say about me, besides synonyms for nice.

I saw Shauna holding Rico's hand, and the churro vendor blew his nose loudly as they carried my body away.

My parents wore colorful clothes, clothes they said I liked, and they were right on that part. I *did* want my death to be a day of happy remembrances, rather than sad losses.

And someone called my name again, and I turned behind me.

The surprise had worn off at this point, and I said hello to my cat.

"Nice to see you again, Joli. I miss the steak breakfasts you fed me." my cat said.

I sat on the grass and pet him, and asked him, "So can all cats talk and see spirits? Would've been helpful to know in the living world."

The cat purred, and said, "All cats. All the time. It's what makes us special, not like those pesky *dogs...* Sure, they can do the same, but we, we have wayyy more lives..."

I said, "That's true. I guess dogs just know when their time's up, while cats know when others' time is up."

The cat hmmed at this, and said, "I miss our philosophical discussions in your apartment, Joli. Even though technically you were only talking to yourself at the time, I enjoyed them despite."

"So what are you going to do now? Did my parents take you in?" I asked him.

"As compassionate as ever, Joli. I figured something out, I always do. The big question is what *you're* going to do. Being a soul binder... Whew. What a task." the cat said.

"I'm really enjoying it so far. Who knew even demons of Hell needed help to find themself? I'm glad I'm part of a greater purpose." I said.

"Speaking of which, you don't mind giving up on eternal Paradise? I'm sure in Heaven you'd have the greatest purpose imaginable." the cat said.

"Nah, I'm sure I landed in Hell for a reason, all part of God's plan, so to speak. I do wish I knew how I got there, though..." I said.

"I'm sure you'll figure it out. You're smart, resourceful, caring, kind, a good friend in all regards, a necessary friend, for one who wishes to see the grand complexity of all life." the cat said.

I said, "The best eulogy I've gotten all day. Thank you, Rasputin."

The cat smirked at me, and said, "Anytime. I'll see you and Hana around, Joli. I miss my past friends and owners, at times... but hardly notably. Take care, Lafaya Joliet Bonaparte."

I then woke up, smiling to myself. What a good guy, my cat.

3

The Half Angel

The wing fitter and the soul binder were as busy as ever, Joli helped all sorts of people find their missing souls, and Tom... had more souls than he could wing fit alone.

37

"We need some vulture wings, some bee wings, and two classics, Belladonna!!" I shouted to the back.

"I'm working, I'm working... Don't rush me! I (cough) am working as fast as I can!!" Belladonna shouted back.

Holly led about two dozen more souls to our office, and I put a hand to my forehead in stress. This was more than I bargained for, being a wing fitter.

I said to Holly, "More?? Where in Heaven are these people coming from! I thought we weren't getting a new transport of souls until Monday!!"

Holly shrugged, and said, "They just poofed! Some angels dropped them off here, and I found 'em!"

"Um. Are my vulture wings ready yet?" a thin old geezer of an angel said to me in the lobby.

"Almost done!" I assured him.

"Good. Such good creatures, vultures. They keep the land clean by devouring roadkill. Always like a clean road..." the old geezer said. He looked more like a buzzard, rather than a geezer, actually...

I got back to my office, and told the young girl we can get back to the wing fitting.

She looked a little scared, and said, "It won't hurt, will it? I don't like operations..."

"I know, Suzy. I'm sure it sucked having them all the time down below, but you won't feel a thing when I attach the wings. Just sit still, right there... and there! Your little gold wings are fit and fine!" I said, smiling after attaching the wings.

She fluttered her gold wings, gasping at them behind her. She jumped off the table, and flew around the room, giggling in delight. I smiled, and said, "Now, I'm supposed to give you a job as well, but I think you'd prefer to go to school like any kid-"

She shook her head at me, up in the air, and said, "No. I wanna be an ankylosaurus! Those have the big clubs on their tails, to ward off predators!"

I scratched my head at her, and said, "Well, since your parents are still alive and well, and you probably won't be seeing them for a while, should I contact one of your other relatives so you don't feel alone in Heaven? What about old Great Grandpa Jack?"

She flew down back to the ground and shook her head at me. She said, "Great Grandpa Jack is scary. He always spit brown blobs everywhere..."

I knelt down before her, and said, "Trust me, he's a good soul, but you don't have to meet him right away, if you don't want to. How about I call a couple I know, and they can take you to see the ankylosauruses in the wilds here. Those dinosaurs are quite breathtaking!"

She gasped in surprise, and said, *"Really??* Are they nice? The people, *and* the dinosaurs??"

I smiled, and said, "The most nice ever, Suzy. Oh! I see the people in the lobby now. Come and meet Nevaeh and Felix."

I took Suzy to the lobby, and she wowed at how big Nevaeh's wings were, and how big Felix was. Nevaeh said, "I got a message from a courier angel to meet you here. What's up, Tom?"

"I still don't know how those courier angels do it, getting the message out before I can even think of what to say... This is Suzy, Nevaeh, Felix. She recently died from lung cancer, and would like someone nice to stay with for awhile." I said.

Nevaeh knelt before Suzy, and offered her arms for a hug with a smile. Suzy ran to Nevaeh's hug, and said, "You look nice."

"I am, Suzy. Let's get you something good to eat, and then-" Nevaeh said.

I whispered, "She likes dinosaurs."

"-and then we'll see the dinosaurs." she finished.

Suzy looked up at Felix, with a big happy smile on both their faces. Felix shook Suzy's hand, tiny compared to his, and Felix said, "Would you like a piggy back ride, Suzy?"

She nodded quickly, still smiling.

Felix hoisted her up, and put her on one broad shoulder, and the three left, waving goodbye to me, smiling in happiness.

The old buzzard geezer said, "So sweet. I knew coming here to get my wings fit was the right choice. Can I have my wings now?"

I smiled, gave the man a wink, and said he's next up.

38

This was an intense quest for a soul.

I had to put a great, evil dictator of history's soul back from pieces, and Dominus and I scoured the Plains of Wrath for the little bits of soul mirror glass, here and there, hidden in the dirt and sand.

The dictator sat back on his horse, a demonic looking thing that actually was his most trusted advisor's soul, transformed into a horse. The advisor had betrayed this dictator, leading to the dictator's downfall, and was now cursed to be forever ridden by his liege. The dictator... did too many horrors to count! Even though the history books looked quite favorable on him, if I remember right from school.

Dominus said, "Oh, Joli! Another bit over here. For such a wicked soul the glass sure shines bright..."

We added the piece of soul glass to the bag, and I said, "We weren't always the horrible monstrosities we sometimes grow into. That dictator was a little baby, at one point of his life, as pure as the rest."

We saw the lumbering demon in the distance, the one we stayed away from on our quest. Some demons, especially ones in the Plains of Wrath, could not be seen reason, and were very dangerous to *any* soul that crossed them. Even Hana couldn't subdue these demons, only fight endlessly against them, which was in fact just what they wanted to do in the afterlife, endlessly fight.

But the lumbering demon, looking like a large ogre with huge horns, finally spotted us.

And then we noticed the sword he was dragging in his left hand.

A sword made of mirror soul glass, the dictator's soul.

It shined so bright, as the ogre demon charged us.

Dominus wielded his own weapon, the only thing he said he had the skill to use properly. An axe to chop wood. Dominus had a very harsh childhood, and he was always sent to use this axe to get more firewood for the woodburning stove.

I held onto my blacksmith's hammer close, a gift from Hana to help me bind souls together.

Dominus dodged the arcing, scything strike of the soul sword, and counterattacked the ogre demon, as the dictator watched from his horse.

The ogre demon grunted in pain as Dominus hacked at his sides, over and over.

It turned to Dominus, about to slice him in half, and I jumped out from hiding and whacked the ogre on the head!

The ogre demon lumbered a few seconds more, and passed out on the ground.

We quickly grabbed the soul sword, and got the Hell out of there.

We arranged the pieces in Hanatrix's castle together, like building a glass mirror puzzle, and soon had a large fractured mirror of a soul.

The dictator watched from beside us.

I then slammed the hammer on the fractured mirror, and it came back from pieces into a full soul.

The dictator looked at the soul mirror, and finally saw himself.

He gasped, as he saw who he really was, and not a demon.

He knelt before us, thanking us for saving his soul, and that it would not go to waste.

He let his advisor free, and the advisor horse ran off into the distance of Hell.

39

I locked up at the end of the day, and Holly, Belladonna and I went to get drinks with Cherry at a pub Cherry liked. We all joked and laughed with each other, us wing fitters, even though we were all very tired.

Belladonna actually was a maker angel. She liked to build stuff, and I think we probably just got off on the wrong foot when we met the first time. There's nothing so nice as learning that someone isn't so bad as you initially thought, and can end up being... a friend.

Holly was a finder angel, through and through. She buzzed with energy, and always seemed so cheerful! Meeting her was a very happy memory for me, and we still whistled when we liked. She actually didn't have a lot of family in Heaven, died young so most were still alive, but was eager to find her ancestors.

Cherry taught us all sorts of things about wing fitting, which people might want new wings or new jobs, how to fit the wings together properly, and even the proper placement based on a person's physiology and stature. There were so many facets of knowledge in these few aspects of wing fitting alone, and she doled out her knowledge gladly, but still I think she just liked having a drink outside of her forest with us younger angels when she could.

We drank at the pub, and Belladonna was asking Holly what it was like to grow up in Heaven.

Holly hmmed, and said, "It's a lot of fun! Almost too fun! Makes me wonder what I was missing in life, sometimes, but... all I can remember from life are the tubes and wires, and then... pop! I was in Heaven."

Belladonna said, "That's (cough) pretty nice of God to give you such a nice home, and even the ability to grow up. Would suck being an eternal kid in Heaven. I nearly hit the big age where you die culturally, 30, but I did the stupid organ selling business. Not like I had much to live for, anyway, but yeah, I guess I wonder what it would've been like to grow old."

I sipped at my delicious, frothy ale, and said, "I died middle age."

Belladonna looked up and down at me, and said, "You don't look a day over twenty! What's the deal, longhair?"

I smiled, and said, "I think this is just how I always imagined myself, or liked to. And don't we all wish we were kids again? I'd say there's nothing wrong with being an eternal kid in Heaven, if God allows it."

Cherry said, "Ah yes... I remember I tried that age, being young, but I took on this age to naturally do my work better. Kids have short, stubby fingers and short, lil' arms... Could hardly sew a wing correctly if I was five, so I take on this age where it's a lady's own secret how old I am..." She laughed uproariously at this.

"One thing I wanted to ask you, Cherry... Why are there so many new souls sent to us? Did some major catastrophe happen, that all these angels need wings, or are we just getting too popular for the workload?" I said.

Cherry said, "You didn't hear? Some poor souls are poppin' down to Hell, and only Hell's Queen and her supporters have been sending them back to us. It's really a mystery, and I asked God personally why he allowed those souls to be taken to Hell... and he simply said that we all find our way in time. Strange man, that God… Makes me feel at ease anyway, because I'm sure he knows what he's doing."

I wondered at this, and we finished our beers and left the pub.

I smoked beside Belladonna outside, as Holly flew and whistled down the street. Who knows where she lived, but I'm sure she'd find a nice bed. Cherry bid us goodnight, and walked off alone into the forest.

40

Hana was always busy, and I asked her at dinner how she does it! She surely can't do the whole job by herself, even if she has Beleth to do grunt work!

Hana sighed out after a long day, and said, "It's tough, I'll give you that, so I make sure to treat myself after a long day. Sometimes I go on long walks in the park, other times I sample local cuisine with a few friendly demons, and other times... Well, sometimes I pray."

I said, "So how did you find God, and why exactly are you blind, if it's ok to ask?"

Hana said, "I saw, and caught, God's beauty myself. I caught the rainbow, and I paid the price. I learned that there's so much beauty to be found, even whilst blind, and I thank God for showing me marvelous creation, even Hell. My mom would've cured me of blindness, but I declined as I would've had to live in Hell to keep my sight. Now, whelp, she's gone, I've had to take up her position and live in Hell anyway, and she can't cure my blindness even if I wanted sight."

"Where do you think she went?" I asked.

"I don't know. I sometimes have vivid dreams of her having tea with strange, tentacled creatures, or popping out of books and talking to the reader and even the writer, but I'm not sure what to make of them.

Kinda weird to think there's other realities out there, and that my mom is just bouncing along through them as she pleases." Hana said.

"So... *are* you and your mom magic? How does one... travel to other realities? I admit it makes me kind of curious." I said.

Hana smiled mysteriously, and said, "You see what's beneath the veil, and continue to read the words between the lines. I used to be able to see past the veil, took a brief glimpse, and I saw too far, so that's how I lost my sight. I can't see... anything, now."

Dominus took a break from slurping down Hana's delectable food, and said, "Oh great Queen, if anyone could do it, it'd be you. What if someone cured your blindness? There are a few demons you could maybe get to do that for you, or have you talked to *God...* and seen if he can?"

Hana said, "Call me Hana, Dominus. We're friends now, I think, although you seem more like my soul binder's hot piece of action over anything long term... I could go to God or demons, but I actually prefer my world as it is, sightless I may be..."

I held Dominus's hand, and said, "I'm glad we're all friends. Dominus has been so helpful to me in finding souls to bind! And really, I feel so safe with him at my side, because there are some *scary* things in Hell, and Dominus... Well, he's probably had sex with about half of them!"

Dominus coughed, and said, "Not... inaccurate..."

I asked Hana, "Say... Do *you* have any romantic interests?? How come the Queen doesn't have a King by now??"

Hana smiled at me, and said, "Well, I'd prefer another Queen to rule by my side, actually."

Dominus gulped another bite, and said, "Like Selma, right? She always gets so flustered when talking about you, your majesty, Hana, even though she tries to hide it when you're around."

Hana rubbed her chin, and said, "Not... inaccurate. I loved a woman for a long time in the living world, and my first true love was a man, an angel of love. They've both gone to Heaven, however, and left their old loves like me in the dust..."

"Can we set you up on a date with one of them?? Dominus and I would go with you, and we'd have so much fun!!"

Hana said, "I think I'd like that very much. I wonder if Sara even-"

Then crack, a strong looking woman, eyes closed, with only a right angelic wing appeared on the table in front of us.

She said, "Give me back my piece of soul, Hana."

And she opened her eyes, and her left eye was blind.

41

I got a call from the herald angel, and he said, "Tom. We're missing a very kind soul, Sara Tobyson, after... she started changing."

I said, "What happened to her? Nothing God can't fix, right?"

"I don't know. I think God would just wave his hands and make things better... but this means something important. Her left wing fell out, and we couldn't figure out how in Heaven to reattach it, and then she started losing her sight. We think she may be going through some crisis of the soul, and urge you to find her and help her, if you can. No one like a good wing fitter to help you fix your soul up." the herald angel said.

I agreed, and said, "Where was she last seen?"

"Actually, she seemed to have been spotted in Purgatory, based on what Paul says. He saw an angel *running* down the fields of Purgatory, and reported it after trying to chase her down himself. Apparently she evaded him, and is on the run still." the herald angel said.

I said, "Ok, I'll check it out myself. I'm sure Belladonna and Holly can do the job of wing fitting without me for a while, and I'll see if Cherry will take my place. I'll talk to you later."

"God's luck on you, Tom." the herald angel said, and hung up.

Cherry agreed to take up my position, I wished Holly and Belladonna good luck, and-

Belladonna wiped the sweat off her brow, and said, "You can't leave me with these schmucks! I'm... not really a people person!"

Holly said, "Oh! I know, I could find you a happier personality!"

Belladonna glared at Holly, as Holly smiled, but Cherry walked in through the doors of our office, and said, "Heya, guy and gals. Let's get to work! Go find that missing angel, Tom! This is exactly what a wing fitter is supposed to do, help the angels find their wings. I'll be rooting for you!"

I smiled, gave Holly a whistle and Belladonna a firm handshake, and Cherry patted my back as I walked out the door, waving them goodbye.

I asked Max for a ride to Purgatory, and he picked me up at the gas station, where I picked out a bunch of snacks and tasty Heavenly delights, with the cashier's help, and put them all in a backpack on my back. The cashier had said, "Nothing like comfort food to warm the soul."

Max picked me up, and I asked him how the work was, and he said, "Eh. It's ok. Been rather peaceful lately, with the whole world peace thing. Now I just worry about the souls like Sara, and the other lost souls, who go places before I even have a chance to seek them out. Wasn't like this in the old days. I could sniff out a dead or dying soul like a basset, but these guys... it's like I'm noseblind."

I asked Max if he had time to help me search for Sara Tobyson, and he accepted. We got to Paul, who was looking annoyed and smoking a cigarette sitting on a bench in Purgatory. Max waved him in the car, Paul got in the back, and we drove down the paths of Purgatory.

Paul said, "I was *this* close to catching her! I know Purgatory like the back of my hand, and having her ditch me at the crossroads somehow really irks me..."

"What would you have done if you *did* catch her?" I asked.

Paul said, "I don't know. Just begged her to come back. I've never seen such a strange sickness of a soul, and I've seen a lot of soulwise unhealthy individuals... It was like... like a piece of her was missing, and continuing to become lost. It wasn't even like a demonic transformation, more like she just wasn't there."

I said, "Hmm... Where can you go, from Purgatory? Only goes to Heaven, am I right?"

Paul said, "Well, the path from Hell is opened to Purgatory, so those demons who do wish forgiveness and repentance have the opportunity to do so, and you can't get here from the living world without an angel of death's help, so..."

"She went to Hell, then. It's the only explanation that makes sense, if she was traversing through Purgatory. But why would *anyone* want to go to Hell?" I said.

Max said, "I don't know guys, but we'll check the dropoff to see what we can find."

We kept driving down the peaceful paths of Purgatory, and soon... got to a large cliff, the dropoff to Hell. I gasped when I saw that awful sight.

42

The half angel seemed to be flickering, almost fading, and she repeated herself, "GIVE ME MY SOUL BACK!! I know you have it, Hana. I knew you... changed, ever since you got to Hell. I KNEW IT!!" The angel then looked at her flickering hands and cried out, "Not again!! Just leave me alone!!"

And she vanished.

Hana screamed out, "SARA!! Please come back! I don't know where your soul is, I can't sense it! Where are you?? You smell like wheat to me! Please come back!"

It was silent. Dominus dropped his fork.

Hana got up frantically, and Beleth caught her before she tripped in her haste. Beleth sniffed in the air, and said, *"Doesn't smell like brimstone, so she's not a demon... What was she, Queen?"*

Hana said, "I don't know, I need to know. I'm going to the Moirai. I'm sure they know, they must know!!"

Beleth said, *"Are you sure? They charge quite a price..."*

"I'll give them Hell, if they ask!! But I need to know Sara is ok!" Hana said.

I said, "W-Wait, Hana. Let me and Dominus look around, while we can. Maybe she didn't go far?"

Hana calmed her breathing, and said, "Ok. I'll give you an hour, before I go to the Moirai. One. Hour."

I nodded my head, said yes, and she charged out the doors to the outer pavilion as Beleth followed her.

Dominus and I inspected the spot where the angel appeared. Dominus said, "Hmm… Doesn't seem like she left even a footprint, eh, Joli?"

"I know… No essence of soul, either… Usually demons are dripping with something, solid, liquid, or even gaseous matter of soul when they're losing their soul. Although… look here, does this pattern look strange to you? The pattern of the tablecloth."

Dominus looked at it, and said, "Huh. It's like the pattern just switched backwards, all of a sudden. Was it always like this?"

"No… I don't think so, but I can't be sure… Maybe there is something with something being reversed here…" I said.

"Well. Let's check around. Perhaps she just went invisible. Demons can do that often, and I'm sure angels can too." Dominus said.

"I don't think so, Dominus. But let's look around." I said.

We searched and searched around the castle, even got the staff to help, but we weren't in time to find anything else concrete before Hana announced she was going to the Moirai.

She said to me, "You're welcome to come along, Joli. I could use the moral support. Please, hold my hands."

I did, and Hana and I traveled by shadow to the Moirai.

So…

…

…Dark…

…The…

…Fate…

…Of…

…Life…

...

I gasped in front of a lamp in front of a shadowy hut, and Hana barged into the hut. I trailed after her, wondering what fate had in store.

43

I noticed something as we looked off the dropoff. There was a picture flying through the wind, almost blowing down to Hell, but caught in my hand before it could be swept away. I looked at the photo, and it was a picture of a young girl... and a song scribbled on the back.

I showed the photo to the others, and Paul said, "That's Sara when she was a child, I can tell. I looked after her and Hana for a good while as a guardian angel, while they were alive... The least I could do for one of my great descendents, and her girlfriend, Sara."

I blinked, and said, "So we're chasing your great, great, great-"

"We're chasing my descendent's past love. We'll leave all the greats out." Paul said.

"...Do you think she went to Hana? Where would Hana be?" I asked.

Paul waved a hand off the cliff, and said, "Down there, ruling over Hell with an iron thumb."

"...Oh. She's *that* Hana. Hanatrix, right?" I said.

Paul nodded.

Max said, "Let's all drive down in the car. We're apparently pretty close, if we're finding belongings of Sara's scattered in the wind."

We got back in the car, and Max revved up his engine.

He slammed on the gas, and we went flying off the cliff to Hell.

We fell for a ways, straight down. The engine stalled.

Max said, "One sec, she does this occasionally... Just my luck, getting stuck with my old junker of a car for my eternity..."

Max tried to start up the pale car, rrr, rrrr, as it failed to turn over constantly.

My heart beat fast. I wondered what dying would feel like now that I was dead?

But the car started, and we swooped away from the ground, flying low through Hell.

We passed into a cave, which bright, happy lights and a sign denoted, "Welcome to Hell! Your Queen's blessings on you!"

We continued to drive down the happy cave, as cheerful music started playing all around us.

Paul said, "...Seems... Hana's redecorated a good deal, in favor of her new dominion..."

Max said, "I always get so damned lost whenever I come here... and I don't know if I'm going through the worst amusement ride, or the best path through Hell..."

I said, "Definitely both. There looks to be a fork in the road..."

We saw a sign that unfortunately was vandalized and now said, *"Beelzebub's Subs! He's the bub with the sub! Get them HOT at the Gluttony Grill!"*

We questioned each other which way to go, and I saw a little demon watching us from the side. I waved at it. It waved back. I rolled down the window, and asked it for directions.

She said, *"That way for big suffering, that way for little!"*

"...What's that mean, again?" I said.

"You want to go big? Or go little?" she said.

I shrugged, thanked her for her help, which she cackled at me and ran off down the "little" path.

Max said, "Go big or go home, right?"

Paul and I shrugged, and Max drove down the big path.

He instantly did a u turn, as millions of chattering, cackling demons chased us from the big path, and we raced back down the little path.

44

There were three spindly, old women cackling at Hana, in an old, filthy hut.

They said, *"So low, to come to the lowest..."*

"So average, to seek for aid..."

"So high, to finally fall..."

Hana said, "Enough, Fates. I know you like to toy with people's lives, and thus you were sent here. But I need to know the answer to Sara's... disappearance. I need to know where she is. And I swear to GOD if you've toyed with her too-"

They said, *"Oh no, Oh Queen..."*

"Oh yes, we did nothing, Oh Queen..."

"But we do know what her fate is, left to the unmaking..."

Hana said, "The unmaking? What does that mean?"

They said, *"Tut, to wish the fate before conception..."*

"Tut, Tut, to dwindle in between..."

"Tut, Tut, Tut, when the end is the beginning..."

Hana said, "...Can you tell me how to stop it? This unmaking? What is it you want from me for this knowledge? I will give it, I swear."

I held Hana's hand and said, "You don't have to give them anything, Hana. Let's go, before their weird riddles hurt our heads too much..."

They said, *"We want one thing, Oh Hanatrix..."*

"We have no other knowledge, but you will listen..."

"You will accept your fate, when the time comes. And you will know what that is."

Hana said, "Very well. I will accept my fate. Good day... crones."

They cackled at us, all three of them, as we left the hut.

We walked through the bog for a while, as will o wisps tempted us to get lost, and I asked Hana, "...So what did you learn, exactly? Seemed like a bunch of gibberish to me."

"Apparently Sara's fate is to be reversed, unmade. A fate worse than death. I don't know what my 'fate' is, exactly... but I'm sure it's not in the hands of those crones. I will always fight for those I hold dear, and I make this fate because I choose it. I do not wait for fate to fall into my lap." Hana said.

"Good. Let's continue to search for Sara. What can you tell me about her? It could give me a clue to find her soul, and how to restore it." I said.

Hana sighed, holding my hand as we walked through the bog. I helped her avoid a giant pothole, and she said, "She was so... *strong*. She was a slave, but she broke her binds and learned and lived despite of the cruel caste she was thrown in. She was... beautiful, not only in sight, but in feeling, caring, and her actions. We spent a long part of life together, before I got the news that my mother had disappeared, and I was expected to take up her role. I've spent a very long time in Hell, longer than you'd expect, but Sara was my end of schoolhood romance in the living world, when we both became full, free thinking adults, and I still look back on those days very fondly."

"That's very sweet. But why was she... so *angry* at you, then?" I asked.

"She never forgave me for leaving her, I think... I don't know how she could expect I'd steal something so precious as her eternal soul, but maybe she was just desperate. I don't think I'd like to be unmade, either." Hana said.

"So what do you think we should do now? I fear to think that Sara is lost in Hell with no one to guide her, being… unmade." I said.

Hana sighed, and said, "Let's go to our local library for information… I have an evil book to check out."

45

We escaped the demons after a good while of them chasing us, and got to a wide open pit of Hell, desolate plains as far as the eye can see.

We stopped by the side of the road, as I saw something alarming.

I saw beautiful feathers, of only an angel would have, I would know, and I saw something beside them...

A human thumb.

I picked up the thumb, which seemed to be flickering, showed it to Max and Paul-

And pop, the thumb vanished.

They were silent, but Max eventually said, "...This isn't good. Angels shouldn't even be allowed to get damaged like that, mutilated, and then..."

Paul said, "Where in bloody Hell did the thumb go?! You don't see angel bits scattered around and disappearing!! It's... unheard of!!"

I looked around the site of the feathers, and noticed red down the path. I quickly raced down the disappearing trail of blood, and yelled at Max and Paul to follow me.

Forward I raced through the wilderness of Hell, down a steep slope, past bramble and dead trees. I saw a flickering form crying by the river of fire, a form with one wing and a blind eye, and I yelled out, "Sara! Sara Tobyson!"

She cowered before me, and I went to her quickly, as she was starting to fade away…

I hugged her immediately, and she lingered in my arms, not disappearing.

Paul and Max came up to us, as I inspected her hand. It was dripping blood from where the thumb was, and Sara explained, "It was starting to disappear, and I thought… if I cut it off, it'd stop the rest of me disappearing again, too… I'm so scared."

I shhed, shhed, and let her cry in terror in my arms.

Max inspected her as well, and said in surprise, "You don't seem… to be an angel anymore. You have human qualities, like… life. This doesn't make sense."

Sara looked up at Paul, as Paul started a cigarette and sat beside us, grim, Sara still in my hug.

Sara said to Paul, "Y-You look just like Hana's father. Are you her father's brother or something?"

Paul said, "No, I'm the Spawn of Sax. Think of me as Hana's grandfather, how about. It'll save time."

Sara continued to cry, and I continued to hold her hand that wasn't mutilated, as Paul bandaged up her bleeding hand with a piece of cloth from his black coat. I took off my backpack, and offered any of its contents to Sara, whatever she liked.

She picked out something I had gotten last minute in the gas station. She picked out potato bread.

Sara said, "This… This is like what Hana and I made on the farm… Potato bread. It's so good, and… nostalgic."

I opened up the package of potato bread, and fed her pieces of bread. She chewed on it slowly, swallowed, and I continued to feed her.

At first it seemed like she was going to vanish if I let go of her, but after I fed her a good bit of potato bread, she seemed much safer in my arms, firmer in reality.

Sara said, "I just don't know why Hana is doing this..."

Paul said, "This isn't Hana's doing, Sara. We'll take you back to Heaven immediately-"

But Sara said, "Please... I just want to see her again, one more time... I just wish none of this ever happened..."

46

Hana asked for a specific book in the library. The librarian said, *"You want that?? ...Ok. Just... don't lose it, damned thing is always appearing in new spots, and I forget where I place it half the time..."*

The librarian then gave Hana the burning book, also known as Satan.

The burning book exclaimed, *"Hana! So nice to... SEE you!! HAHA-HAHA... Not like you can even read my words!! Whatcha doin' at the library, anyway? Here to pick up chicks?"*

Hana said, "No, I simply came to ask you a few questions. You have such knowledge, being one of the oldest demons in creation... yet instead you lie and use deceit, or even try to make ill mannered jokes."

"Oooh did I hurt the wittwe pwincess's feewings? And why the heck did you bring a soul binder with you? Come to save my soul again, have you?" the burning book said.

I said, "...You know about soul binders?"

"All sorts of things about souls. It's how I made a living, stealing the lives and souls of mortals... I just took the knowledge of soul binding, and did the opposite, starting with Adam and Eve themselves..." the burning book said.

I said, "Would you be able to help us return a soul from being... unmade? Do you even know what that is?"

The burning book said, *"What's it worth to you? Is it worth... oh... my own form back? I would intensely love to see my EVIL image in a mirror again..."*

Hana said, "No, it's not worth allowing you freedom from the burning book. But it is worth a nice, shady spot in Beleth's library, next to his naked lady magazines..."

The burning book paused, and sighed. He said, *"I really hate getting the short end of a deal. You better stick me next to the 2022 catalog, that one's my favorite. To answer your question, I have only heard of the sort of thing, unmaking, when people in the living world decide they dislike something in their past history SO much, that they cut it out, and basically... unmake it! Pitiful creatures, humans, can't even take pride in their past..."*

Hana said, "...So... It's someone from the living world doing this?"

"Oh... Probably everyone... Someone who intensely disliked you so much, Hanatrix, that they wished to cut you out of their life..."

Hana smiled, and said, "That's where your lies come up short, Satan. I am not being unmade, but my love is, and doubt very much anyone would want to forget Sara. I believe I found a *smidgen* of truth in your words, and I don't want you anywhere near me in the castle, so you will be rewarded with a *smidgen* of what I promised. Librarian? Could you categorize this book as smut, and have it placed accordingly?"

The burning book stuttered out, saying, *"No! I know it's someone after you! Probably that pesky God, of course!! Believe me, pleeeeease!!"*

Hana handed the book to the librarian, the librarian shrugged, and placed the burning book in the smut category.

The burning book actually seemed quite pleased, as we walked out of the library, and was practicing his pick up lines on the naked lady magazines.

I asked Hana, "...So... Don't trust that guy, got it. What did we *actually* learn?"

Hana said, "Apparently this is a wish come true, and I do not believe unmaking is the wish of *others* but rather the wish of *oneself.* I believe Sara wishes she could reverse a lot of things, and wishes to change her... fate. We just have to tell her this, and somehow make her come to peace. Where do you think she'd be, Joli?"

I looked up, seeing a pale, flying car going in the direction of the castle, and I said, "I don't know, but those guys in the flying car probably know. Let's go home."

47

This extremely happy, extremely bubbly, young woman was shaking my hand like I was someone she always wanted to meet, and strangely... also knew my name.

"TOM!! I'm so happy you're real!! I *knew* drawing lets you see the truth!! So delighted to meet you, mister angel! I'm Lafaya Joliet Bonaparte, but *you* can call me Joli! What kind of angel are you?? I'm a soul binder!!" the woman, Joli, said.

I smiled, as she continued to shake my hand, and said, "I'm a wing fitter. Are you a demon? You don't look in the least like one!"

She said, "Oh, no, I never cared for the whole becoming a demon thing. I guess you'd just call me a spirit. That's Dominus, over there, and he used to be the most lustful incubus in all of Hell, but I bound his soul back together for him! (He's now the most lustful spirit in all of Hell, but keep that between you and me!)" The young man waved to me, giving me a charming smile.

Sara was sitting with Hana as Hana fed her soup, with Paul and Max sitting opposite them at the table. Sara just mumbled, "I just wish... I wish we could go back in time, start over, never go in this direction..."

Hana just told her to shush, and continued to feed her soup.

Paul said, "So how do we do this, Hana? I've often wished I could've changed my past, but it doesn't help to wish. Maybe she could go through Purgatory, to get rid of the sins that are bothering her? I'd watch over her the entire journey."

Max said, "And... I don't mean to alarm you, but you being... somehow alive, doesn't fit right, Sara. You actually seem like you're a third alive, a third unmade, and a third dead, if that makes any sense, caught between the worlds of past, present, and future. What do you want to do, Sara?"

Sara mumbled, "I want to go back to the farm with Hana... live with our family we made there... or even just back to school with Lux... I miss that robot, like I miss you, Hana... all of our friends..."

And the other wing of Sara's started wilting, the feathers falling off gently. Hana stroked the wing, and cried gently. Hana said, "I do too, Sara. I don't know where Lux is, but all of our friends are up in Heaven, right?"

Sara sniffled, and said, "Yeah, we still have meetings of the Champions of the Gargoyle, but without you... it's just not the same..."

Joli said, "We need to bind her soul, quickly, so she holds onto what she has left. Do you have anything important from your past that I could use?"

Sara reached into her pocket, and said, "Oh... it disappeared, too..."

I picked out the photo in my pocket, and gave it back to Sara. She smiled, looking at it.

"Cockadoodle doo... and the cow goes moo... Our favorite song, Hana." Sara said.

Hana smiled, and said, "It's *so* cool you finally learned that Toby was really your real father, after all that time. Must've been quite a shock meeting him in Heaven, eh?"

Sara shook her head, and said, "He was the first one waiting at the gate for me, side by side with... your dad. Your father actually explained that he forgave Toby's misfire which killed him, and I was so happy to meet your dad, too..."

Hana said, "He popped by to visit recently, and I never felt more happy to see my relatives again. You too, Paul! You look just like my dad. The similarities are astounding!"

Paul smiled.

Joli sat on the other side of Sara, and touched the picture gently. Joli said, "Perfect. This picture has a strong tie to you, I can tell. But you never needed it to hold onto yourself. Why not, instead of remembering the past you wish you had, you think about all the stuff in the future you could do?"

Sara said, "I don't know what I want to do. I spent forever in Heaven trying to make an afterlife I could be proud of, but the wish for my life gone just got stronger and stronger."

Hana said, "What if... you and I, Sara... had a picnic? Like we did in the old days? And then we can... like in the old days..." Hana continued to whisper in Sara's ear, and Sara giggled.

I inspected Sara's back, and said, "I think I could make you some even better wings, if you'd like. All I'd need are... feathers! Anything will do, for this scenario."

Hana said to the demon standing at the ready, "Beleth! Grab up any pillows, mattresses, whatever has feathers with the rest of the staff, and bring them here!"

Beleth bowed, said, *"At once, your Majesty..."* and carried out the order.

48

Tom worked so quickly on the wings! We ripped and tore the pillows and mattresses open, and piled their contents before the wing fitter!

Pretty soon, he had two makeshift wings, a right and a left wing, that were red, white, brown, black, all sorts of colors made from insides of furniture.

I said to Sara, "Please, allow me to hold onto the picture for a moment."

Sara looked like she didn't want to let the picture go, but gently handed it to me.

I waved a hand over the photo, and the photo went blank, leaving a filmy pure substance on my hand.

Sara gasped, and said, "*What* have you *done??* That- That photo was my entire past life!! How *dare* you-"

I then quickly touched her forehead with the substance, and the eye that was blind regained its color.

She put a hand over her eye, and said, "I-I can see. I can see with both eyes again."

I held the hand with the missing thumb, unwrapped the bandage, and when I opened my hand from hers, her hand was whole again. She gasped, and said, "I've never seen something like this in all my afterlife. You said you were a soul binder?"

I nodded sweetly, then Tom went to Sara's back and he said, "Ok... be still now..."

And with a quick motion, the wings were attached to Sara's back!

She stood up, looking firm in her being, in her position, and unfurled her wings, looking majestic, and pure, an angel of Heaven. I wowed at such beauty.

She knelt before Hana, and said, "I've always loved you, Hana... I know those times are gone forever. But... I can still visit, can't I?"

Hana looked kinda at Sara, and said, "Always. There's always a special place in my heart for you, my love. Now let's go have that picnic! You gotta see what my kitchen can make! And there's this grotto in Hell where the wind just feels like it lifts you straight up to Heaven..."

Sara helped Hana up from sitting, and the two held hands, going to the kitchen to pack their picnic.

Max said, "Well... All's well that ends well. So... What do you guys want to do? I've probably got to get back to being an angel of death, and Paul probably has to help more people through Purgatory. What do you want to do, Joli?"

I said, "I think I'd love to spy on her majesty and see how the picnic goes!! I've never seen her so buoyant, and... in love! I gotta get, like, a telescope or something-"

Tom said, "How about you leave them some privacy, Joli. I was actually wondering if you'd like to come meet some people in Heaven with me. A soul binder... Wow! Could come in handy with all sorts of people who might be going through the same thing Sara went through!"

I looked at him quizzically, and asked, "...I can take Dominus along, can't I?"

Tom looked at Dominus, who looked surprised, and Dominus said, "B-But g-go to Heaven? You know me, Joli, I-I'm a brave s-soul... but that scares me."

I smiled at him, "Only for a visit. I'd love to meet this God fellow I'm always hearing about! You'll be able to take care of Hana, right, Beleth?"

Beleth shrugged, and said, *"I think Hana would prefer to look after herself, with Sara, for the time being. If you're wondering if Hell will go to pieces without you, just know we've been caring for ourselves for a lot longer than your entire existence, without a frankly very much too nice soul binder hanging around..."*

I laughed, and said, "That's true! Well, let's go, Dominus! I can't wait!"

Tom said, "I actually would like to talk more about the lost souls, if we can get a chance. You might know more about them, right?"

I held Dominus's hand, as he practically shook in anticipation, as we were going to the pale flying car, and said to Tom, "Maybe? I'm actually one of them! We'll figure it out together."

We all got in the car, Paul, Max, Tom, Dominus and I, and took off through the skies of Hell, me giving directions here and there, and flew through the afterlife to Heaven.

4

Where Dinosaurs Go

The wing fitter and the soul binder were dropped off in Heaven. I decided to invite them to dinner and drinks.

49

Joli and Dominus were wowed as all Heaven when we got to the hotel. I told them, "Now, just check in, and then we'll be visiting my friend the herald angel, for dinner! And thanks for helping me show them around, Belladonna."

Belladonna huffed, carrying the bags of souvenirs Joli got, and she said, "I didn't sign up for this shit. Why didn't you get Holly to do this crap?"

"You know, Belladonna, Holly just found the primordial root of her family tree, and is celebrating the old ways with him and his tribe! It's a fantastic moment for her." I said.

"Well, Tom, just cuz I don't have a life doesn't mean I got to do all the dirty work! Set this here?" Belladonna said, in Joli and Dominus's room.

Joli nodded, and said, "Thank you so much, Belladonna! I *love* that name! I bet we're going to be great friends in no time!"

Belladonna dropped the bags to the floor, and I said to Joli and Dominus, "Meet us outside when you can. Wear whatever you like!"

Joli said, "We will! Shopping here was *sooo* much fun!! Is it even shopping if everything is free? Oh well! We'll get freshened up, and meet you downstairs!"

Belladonna and I took the elevator, in silence.

We walked through the lobby, in silence.

We stood outside, smoking cigarettes, in silence.

She held my hand, in silence.

I jumped, and she looked deep into my eyes, in silence.

She said, "I kinda... I don't know. But I think I like you, longhair."

I sighed, but smiled nicely, and said, "I think I could like you too, Belladonna... It's just- I have a wife."

She opened her eyes in surprise, and slowly... let go of my hand.

I tried to explain, "I promised her I would wait up for her in Heaven... and I intend to keep that promise. I'm sorry, Belladonna."

Belladonna smiled sadly, and said, "My luck. All the good guys, even in Heaven, are taken..."

I smiled sadly as well, but still offered my arms open for a hug.

She hugged me close and nice, then broke off, looking into my eyes nicely.

I said, "You're still welcome to come to dinner and drinks with us."

"Nah, I was really hoping it was a date, so now that I know it's not, I'm going to blow you off and watch tv, eating ice cream in my pajamas. It's my favorite hobby. Well. I'll see you at work, longhair... Tom." she said, and jumped into the air, flying away on purple wings, not looking back once.

I opened my eyes wide as Joli and Dominus came down, Joli wearing a rainbow dress, shimmering every which way, and Dominus wearing the most dashing suit I had ever seen.

We walked to the bus, and I took a seat. Joli asked the bus driver, "If everyone can fly, why does Heaven need a bus?"

The bus driver looked at Joli stonily, and said, "I s'pose for people like you. Some people just like taking the bus. Don't gotta flap around, don't gotta get lost."

Joli said, "That makes sense! Thank you!"

Joli from force of habit was going to take out fare, but stopped as she was doing so and instead gave the bus driver a nice handshake. The bus driver shook her hand back gladly.

We got to the restaurant, an al fresco place, and I saw the herald angel... with two lady angels I had seen before.

Yule the seraph was wearing pure white pants and an open blouse, and Jane the angel of Hell was wearing a short, black skirt and sporting a jean jacket. The herald angel was wearing a grey hoodie and jeans, casual I suppose.

I looked at my corduroys and dress shirt, and I felt sort of overdressed, especially with Joli in that stunning dress and Dominus in that dashing suit.

Joli and Dominus didn't care, though. They seemed to like being the big shots, enjoying their trip to Heaven. I introduced them to the three, and we sat down with them at the table.

The herald angel said, "Weren't you bringing a plus one, Tom?"

I said, "Er, she changed her mind."

The herald angel shrugged, and ordered a round of beers for all of us.

I wondered at the herald angel's actual relationship with these two women, and what they were doing here. I expected another big, booming bold voice command or quest, but it seemed like the three just wanted to hang out. I suppose they all were friends-

The herald angel kissed each of the ladies, on the lips, as they kissed him longly back, and I suddenly knew relationships in Heaven were a little stranger than advertised from sermons.

50

Oh! So they were a love trio! That's so cool! I only really heard of things like that, but I suppose anything is possible in Heaven!

It *did* kind of surprise me, seeing even the two ladies hold each other's hands longingly, but Dominus seemed completely comfortable with this!

Dominus whispered to me, "The guy is their buffer, y'know the one they can bounce back to for anything, the albino is the strongarm tough chick, probably the powerhouse in bed, and the blonde one... I think she keeps things fun and interesting."

I whispered, "Ohhhh! How do they- What about-"

The herald angel winked at me, and I gulped.

Dominus burst out laughing, and Tom was drinking heavily, ordering another beer, and another beer. We decided to skip dinner, and just enjoy the evening with drinks. I had already eaten so much already, as soon as I got here! Heaven food is *amazing!*

We were walking down to the sea of Heaven, and I was like, Heaven has a sea? But the herald said, "The seas of Heaven come and go, but it's where some angels feel the most at home."

We walked down by the beach, Tom stumbling, and saw a few naked skinny dipping angels! They waved to us, and we waved back!

Tom mumbled, "I'dddd... throw up, if it waaaas possssibleeee... but thissss alcoooooohol, just makes my stomach feel... *better.* I miss... my wife..."

I patted him on the back, as he had a melancholy look on his face, and to cheer him up I said, "I know! Let's go swimming, like those skinny dippers! The bright moon over the sea... The water just looks so pleasant!"

Dominus immediately ripped off his suit and dove into the water. I was next, dropping my dress, and chased him! The love trio decided to sit on the sand with Tom, smoking cigarettes, but I was having fun with Dominus in the water. We dove, we swam, we laughed and played... and we kissed, naked bodies against each other in the water, with the full moon shining down on us... This was probably the best vacation of my entire- afterlife.

We got out, finding two, folded, very convenient, dry towels waiting for us, with our names embroidered on them, and dried ourselves off and got dressed, walking back to town.

We found a live band playing in the park, and we all danced together! I wondered how the love trio would dance, but they either all boogied together, politely traded off... or even danced with me! The albino woman was so much fun! She seemed like no matter what, if she was around I'd be safe. Jane and the herald angel danced a slow dance, and it looked like a very intimate moment.

Yule, the albino woman, urged Tom, who was stumbling around, to play something for us! She said to him, "I heard you could also be an angel of music! C'mon, everyone give a hand for TOM!"

The people all cheered him onto the stage, and Tom shrugged, smiled, and went up front, which the guitarist gave him the guitar.

And Tom played and sang.

Wooooooooow. I never knew the wing fitter knew so much, in such a musical way.

I danced in a lively way with Dominus, as Tom seemed to play his entire repertoire of music, the band playing with him fantastically. I looked at the love trio, and Yule had her arms around each of her mates, as they sat on the bench and listened to the music. The herald angel had an arm around her waist, and the angel of Hell had a hand on her thigh.

I looked up at Tom, and he was smiling, content, finally.

51

I stumbled to my bed in the Heaven hotel… I was *exhausted.* Relaxing, if you do it right, really takes a lot out of you…

I fell asleep as soon as my head hit the pillow.

In a dream I wondered about my wife, who was still alive. Would she move on after my death? Find another husband? That would seemingly make things complicated.

But I fell to the floor in a church, and I saw her talking with the priest. That no good priest… lucky he was chaste, because every woman, no matter what, had their eyes on him.

I listened, as the rest of the flock filed out. She seemed a little happier after his words.

Was she moving on? Did I mean anything to her, now that I was dead, or was I just a depressing memory?

I got into her car, as she drove home, and she looked at me, straight in the eyes, for just a moment, and then shook her head, shaking me off.

I walked to… my old home.

I saw her work in the garden. She never liked gardening, so I wonder what had changed.

I sighed, seeing her in the sunlight, wiping off the sweat from her brow. I followed her inside, and she had coffee for one.

I saw my pictures hanging up on the wall. I suppose then I must really be gone, if I was only these pictures to her.

She sipped on her coffee, and she broke down crying.

I said, "It's ok. I'm right here."

She continued to cry, and I felt sad.

I wished I could just hug her, to touch her, to let her know it's ok.

I reached out a hand tentatively to her, and brushed against her arm.

She looked up from crying, into my sympathetic eyes.

I woke up, and disappeared from the house.

I just stared up at the ceiling of the hotel, and then went out to the balcony in the middle of the night for a cigarette.

I jumped as someone said from above me, sitting on the rooftop, "Hard night, Tom?"

I looked up, and saw the angel of Hell, Jane, her short skirt being blown in the wind.

She jumped down to the balcony with me, and I offered her a cigarette. She took the cigarette, and lit it with flame coming from her hand.

"How'd you do that…?" I asked.

"Magic. Here, let me help you." she said, and lit my cigarette from the flame coming from her fingertips.

I said, after we stood smoking for a second, "*Why* is life so god-damned *difficult.* Even in the afterlife, in literal Heaven, I still feel sad, and I still feel powerless. I can't do anything for the people I love, no matter how much I want to. It makes me… so very frustrated."

Jane said, "That's a good feeling to have, and you should always cherish that strength, the ability to feel sad. Some people *do* wish they could just wash away all emotion, and some actually succeed. I understand feeling powerless. In Hell, used as a toy by Satan… I felt powerless every single day. My boyfriend and girlfriend try to help where they can… but that powerless, sad feeling remains."

I said, as she was looking sadly out to the horizon of Heaven, "...I'm sorry."

"It's ok. I mean, it's not, and will never be… but it is passed. I suggest you keep pushing through life, or the afterlife, no matter how hard you feel like giving up. If you hope things get better, sometimes they have the power to actually do so. Something my boyfriend said to me, and it stuck with me." Jane said.

I said, "Thank you, Jane. I'll keep pushing for all the souls of Heaven."

"Do so at least for yourself, first. I'll see you around, Tom. The night is young… and I have some good lovin' waiting for me." Jane said.

I smiled, and said, "Thank you for helping me in my worst, as an angel of Hell."

She smiled back, and said, "I'd just say as a friend from now on. Goodnight, Tom."

She then leapt off the balcony, fell a good ways, as I looked down, and she swooped away from the street at the very last second.

52

Dominus and I just couldn't get enough of lovin' each other, in literal Heaven. The sheets were *so* soft.

We had the third round, and I felt up for one more. Dominus had an *inexhaustible* amount of energy.

He taught me some new things, too! Well, pretty much everything was new for me, but things I'd never heard of, even in porn! We switched roles, roleplayed, and I even got to use some cute little handcuffs Dominus had packed!

I, finally, felt oh so *fulfilled,* and got a text from Yule, the seraph. I had exchanged numbers with all of them before we went our separate ways.

Oh, she was just asking if everything was alright for us in Heaven, if we felt safe and all that. She said usually it was against her better nature to allow nearly *anyone* from Hell to Heaven, but from the night we showed her, said I was "cool."

I giggled, and said she was cool, too! I said she'd love to come down and have a party in Hell with us! We could really have a blast, and Hana would be there, too!

She said she'd like that, but… had enough memories of demons and Hell for a lifetime. She had warred for a long time against the infernal forces of the underworld, and decided she'd prefer life in Heaven again.

I asked her what she meant, and she said it was a long story, filled with action, romance, and adventure.

I oooohed at that, and we soon were texting all night.

That Yule Tidings! A gladiator, an angel of war, a seraph!! She inspired me with her story, and made me think that... being a part of a Heavenly organization wouldn't be half bad.

She offered me a meeting with God, at some point.

I said sure! Right away!!

She just said, then, I would meet him on God's Time. Something her boyfriend had thought of recently, meaning that all coincidence, fate, and all outcomes happened on God's Time, even though we eternally have free will.

I said I liked that! I suppose I just landed in Hell on God's Time! It made me feel better, and not so shunned from God, knowing that it was invariably part of his plan.

Yule sent me a smiley face, and said we'd talk more about that later.

I sent her a smiley face back, and a goodnight!

I put my Hellphone back on the side table, and snuggled up with Dominus, who was all tuckered out and sleeping like a babe... So cute!

In the morning, Tom had to go back to work as a wing fitter, and promised that I'd be able to see his job soon, and even help! He told us to go and enjoy the wildlife. "Something spectacular, you'd never, ever believe." Tom had said.

We ate breakfast, devouring pancakes, waffles, strawberries, blueberries, sausage, bacon, all that! I learned that meat in Heaven was actually synthetic, and I could see how this was efficient, as well as humane! It sure didn't taste like any meat I'd ever eaten, it tasted better!

Dominus and I walked down the street to the forests, and gasped as we saw a literal ankylosaurus cross our path.

53

Belladonna seemed to get caught dazing off, strangely. I'd ask her if she was ok, and she'd say, "Hm? Oh, yes, Tom. I'm fine. You said you needed a few sporty wings? Sleek and slender? I'll get right on it."

She wasn't complaining. She was doing her job well. I just didn't know what the heaven was wrong then. Was it something to do with me?

Holly was wearing warpaint from her long lost ancestors, whistling in delight and doing other things around the office, watering the plants, categorizing the files. She had found a sizable amount of unique material from her tribe, and we'd never run out of ceremonial beads and tribal feathers now, unless we were lucky.

I asked her if the trip was everything she hoped, and she spoke in Simbali to me, and strangely… I could understand it!

I spoke in Simbali back, and she smiled, bowed slightly, and said in Simbali, "My gift to you, Tom. I knew I could help you find other languages. Some angels do the hard bits to learn a language, something about enjoying it, but now we have a secret language!"

I laughed, and said in Simbali, "That's so cool! You find so many unique and awesome things, every day!"

She said, "That's my job!"

Belladonna was looking at us funny, and said, "...What's with the gobbledygook?"

Holly and I laughed, and continued talking about her great ancestor, the start of her family tree. Eventually, as Belladonna sighed, and left the wings on my desk, I asked Holly in Simbali, "...Do you know what's wrong with Belladonna? I had to turn her down the other night, and I fear she might have taken it hard..."

Holly looked at me sympathetically, and said in Simbali, "That's ok. I think it's just hard for her to make friends, even though everyone is so awesome and friendly here. I keep asking her to hang out, but she always declines on frankly the saddest excuses! I *know* reading in your underwear is fun, but you don't need to do so every night!"

I said in Simbali, "What if we planned a surprise for her? Something to let her know that she is our friend, no matter what? She was one of the first angels I met in Heaven, and I think of her as a close companion."

Holly shrugged, and said, "I think she thinks of you as one too. I'll go find an idea!! Work on the wings, and let me do my job, busy, busy, busy, comin' through!!"

Holly fluttered away on her canary wings, and I got back to attaching the wings to the next client.

Nevaeh, Felix, Suzy, and someone else decided to visit me. Great Grandpa Jack came in, holding Suzy's hand, smiling in happiness.

54

Dominus and I talked with a few nature angels! The woman, Fate, walked on the grass barefoot as flowers sprung behind her, and Lucius, the man in the tree playing the flute, had animals all around listening to him play.

Lucius hopped out of the tree after his song was finished, pet a polar bear on the head, and smiled to us.

Fate gave us a gift of everliving flowers, blooming before our very eyes.

"Wow! Whatcha guys doin' out here, so far out in the forest?? I just- I just feel like saying wow all the time here! I'm gonna say it a bunch, to get it out of my system. *Wow! Wow! WOOOOW!"* I said.

Lucius said, "Fate and I are simply enjoying the woods. We keep tabs on it, as well as the nature in the living world. I am always busy down below, trying to get nature to thrive... But I spend time for those who matter, like Fate."

Fate said, "I am so happy to meet other angels of nature in Heaven. It can be a very difficult task, protecting nature, and we need all the allies we can get."

Lucius sighed out, and said, "I do wish Yule would've kept to her word to help me... She's been getting so odd lately."

I said, "...Yule? Were you two close?"

Lucius said, "Very, but I think I prefer exploring my options. Yule is the kind of lady that you still love even after the time has passed, and you accept that love, and are also able to let it go."

I nervously said, "...So... You found another love, somewhere, right? I'd hate to think... someone *like you...* was all alone! You're so gorgeous!!"

Lucius smiled at me, scratched his chin, and said, "Lucky for me, I get that a lot. Don't worry about me, miss."

Fate laughed, and said, "If only you spent more time with the ladies, instead of the woods, Lucius..."

Lucius shrugged, and said, "Mother nature will always be my first love, and I am always content in her caring arms."

We talked a bit about how the nature of the living world was inevitably being depleted, and even though we had world peace, drastic measures needed to be taken to save the environment. If only I or someone else could tell the living world this...

We waved them goodbye, and the two continued to walk the woods, one with plants springing to greet her, the other with animals of all types making way for him and following his path.

Dominus and I checked the map, and said we should be able to get back to the hotel if we took this path.

We walked for so long, but felt so energetic and spritely! Something about seeing such beauty, always in nature, really puts a bounce in your step.

We saw a brilliant, pure patch of sunlight on open grass... so soft, inviting... Dominus and I looked deep into the other's eyes, and knew what we wanted to do in this peaceful, secluded spot...

55

All and all it was a good day, an efficient day, despite Belladonna's spirit being so low. I only heard *one* cough from her. One!

Holly sneakily unloaded a bunch of boxes into a room in the back. Asking her what they were, she shushed me, and said they were a surprise.

The day was over, we actually finished up early, and Belladonna sighed and said she was going to go home and draw a new life for herself. She said, "I'm actually thinking of moving, Tom."

I said, "C'mon, no need for that! Come in the back, I have something to show you." I said, hoping Holly's surprise was ready.

Belladonna sighed, but followed me to the back, where Holly unpacked one of the boxes, and took out... clay?

Belladonna looked at the clay, and said, "So... cool. This clay looks like it's good quality. I could make all sorts of nice things with this, I suppose. This is nice, Tom, Holly."

Holly said, "And there's so much more artist supplies for you! I found 'em! Easels, paints, markers, sharpies, colored pencils, crayons, pastels, pretty stones, stickers..."

Belladonna smiled, and said, "I always wanted to be a great artist in my life. Never got the chance to be recognized, but-"

Holly said, "That's where you're wrong! That one painting of yours, I found out, the one painting, with the jackal woman making love to an angel...? That's going on display in a museum, soon! They say your artistry shows a bleak, fantastical part of the world, so real and strange, but so vivid and enchanting to the eyes! And your parents are looking through all your other past work, finally appreciating them, like everyone is doing for the rest of your art!"

Belladonna smiled wide, a big happy smile, and said, "I was on soooo many uppers when I painted 'The Fucking Jackal.' I thought it'd be too rude to ever be put on display... Cool. Death of an artist, eh? Soon as I die people think I'm amazing..."

I said, "We think you're amazing too, Belladonna. Would you mind doing our portraits sometime? That way we always have something to remember you by, no matter where your path in Heaven takes you."

She looked at us, smiling with tears in her eyes, and said, "Sure. I'm (cough) gonna (cough) cry now."

Belladonna burst out crying happily, and Holly and I hugged her close.

We took the art supplies back to her studio apartment, and Holly watched as Belladonna painted my portrait.

"More skin, Tom, less longhair in your eyes." Belladonna said.

I stopped smiling, and took off my shirt?

She frowned at me, and I sighed and got nude.

She nodded, content, and painted me naked as a babe. Holly said, "Me next!! I want a *tribal* looking painting!!"

I wowed as I saw the painting of myself. I looked so intense, in such a kind way. She really captured my long hair well, fwooshing down from my body like the waves of the sea, and was quite generous to the nude parts, accurate despite.

Holly got a fierce picture of her as a woman of an ancient tribe, despite having the biggest smile… with fangs.

"Like a wolf! AWESOME!" Holly said.

Belladonna later painted two portraits of herself for us, and I hung up my paintings in my hotel room, with the signature *Belladonna* on each.

56

We actually got kind of lost, after being so disoriented from great sex! We wandered down the path, and I told Dominus I think we took a wrong turn. Dominus pointed at the distance, however, and said, "...Is that…?"

I squinted, and I saw… a robot? He was looking at some signs, and we ran up to him.

He was muttering to himself. He looked humanoid, with one crystalline eye on his face. He said, "...Is this some sort of virus…? Or… I could've sworn I was deleted, scrapped, and gone for good…"

I said to him, "Hiya, mister! Whatcha doin' out here? We're kinda lost, do you know which way is back to town?"

The robot looked at me, and said, "Hmm. Hi there, human. At least humanity hasn't changed, despite every bit of setting I am accustomed to being different. I saw *dinosaurs* walking around. Is this some sort of odd glitch?"

"No, I don't think so. My name is Lafaya Joliet Bonaparte! Call me Joli. That's Dominus, the sexy man with the sexy plan. Hmm… The sign says go that way, so that's where I think we should go! Care to join us, robot?" I said.

The robot looked at me offering my hand to shake, and shook my hand with WOAH a grip that could crush skulls! He said, "My name's

Lux. Nice to meet you. You actually remind me of a past student of mine who also had an odd name, a girl by the name of Hanatrix."

"You know Hana?? I'm actually her official soul binder!! Dominus and I are on vacation, in this eternal Paradise!" I said, as us three walked down the path.

"...Eternal Paradise...?" Lux said.

"Well, yeah! Where else do you think dinosaurs go when they die?" I said.

Lux paused, and strangely, started laughing, and laughing, in joy.

He said, "I can't believe it! You smartass God... You bastard in... here! I just... Is this happiness, I feel?? I don't think I've ever felt this feeling so well in all my life!! I... HOOOHOO! I'm just so happy!!"

Lux did a little jig in the middle of the path, and we watched him quizzically.

He sighed out in happiness, and said, "I think... OH, whatever... I think I love this place, already! I could study just the... *dinosaurs* for a few eternities more!! Where *are* we going, anyway, Joli?"

I said, "Well, it's sort of a center Heavenly hub, connected to the rest of Heaven through roads and pathways, some hidden except to the most adept, like the ones who can take airways through the clouds, to the others like a normal bus route."

"Let's go, and see this enchanting place! When I see God... I'm going to punch him! You don't save a robot's soul, that's not even supposed to exist! I'm going to wallop that God, for skewing off every bit of belief I ever had!" Lux said, laughing.

Dominus and I shrugged and followed Lux the robot, as he led the way with the walkiest walk!

57

In the lobby of the hotel, Yule was questioning me more about what happened to Sara, and also querying about the lost souls, when Joli, Dominus, and a... robot? Walked in.

Yule gasped, almost was hyperventilating in excitement, and ran to the robot, and gave him a huge hug.

She cried out, "*LUX!!* I knew you had a soul, see, I told you!! I *knew* it!!"

She then started crying in happiness as the robot patted her back.

The robot, Lux, said, "And I'm so happy I do, Yule. Angels! Real, honest to god, angels! I don't know what to make of this place, at all! All I can say is that I am very happy."

Yule took Joli, Dominus, and Lux to the table, and introduced Lux to me.

Lux said, "...A wing fitter? No thanks for me. I don't think I'd like to swoop around like a flighty bird."

I said, "...Really? Most angels want wings. I don't know about myself personally, however."

Yule just said, "So, Lux, tell me everything! What have you been *doing* in life??"

Lux said, "Oh, you know, watching humanity rise and fall, continuously throughout the eras, teaching the remnants of them about their past. I was very happy with my work recently, but just because we have 'world peace' doesn't mean that there isn't still strife... A ruthless corporation wanted my experiment for themselves, a self replicating food that is impossibly cheap to make. I, unlike that silly world peace man, had created a lasting solution to world hunger. I had felt the virus overtaking me, a simple, dominating virus that must've taken years to produce, hand crafted for me. I then, before my entire programming and all my backups could be deleted, fried, and wiped for good, uploaded the formula to... one of my scientific rivals. She will be the woman that humanity accredits to their saving, not that I mind. The work was its own reward."

Yule said, with tears in her eyes, "And yet you have been rewarded again, dear good *soul.*" She wiped the falling tears out of her eyes, and said, "Please, come to dinner with the rest of the people you've helped in your long *life,* Lux. We all wish to thank you for your inspiring presence, guiding hand, and infallible might. We will have a banquet, in your honor, Lux."

We cheered for Lux, and Yule took out her prayer phone and called practically everyone she knew.

There was soon a grand banquet in the lobby of the hotel, with so many people congratulating Lux, in happy reunion with him, or just enjoying the party.

At the end of the long night, Yule hugged Lux one more time, and I showed Lux to his room, with a stumbling Joli and Dominus who were giggling from all the booze they drank.

I said to Lux outside of his room, "This is a home for you, anywhere in Heaven. It's my job to offer you a job, as a new angel, but based on all the people you've helped already, I don't think you need me to tell you what to do."

"...I can go anywhere? Do anything?" Lux asked.

"Whatever you please, in the realm of possibility in Heaven, which is always new and surprising, every day." I said.

Lux pondered for a second in the hall, and said, "I would like to play chess. I know that's kind of cliche for a robot to say they want to play chess, but... I think I'd just like to relax, for a while, and then go back to learning and teaching all that there is to know. Teaching is something that gave my life purpose, and having the free will to do so *always* makes me feel like that purpose was gratified. Good night, Tom."

I bid him goodnight, watched Joli and Dominus stumble into their room as they giggled, and I went to my room.

I admired my paintings again. Every time I looked at them I saw a little detail that I seemed to have missed, and I could tell that Belladonna really did care about me in a grand way. I admired the portrait of her, and sighed out, content.

Dominus and Joli were at it again in the next room, louder than ever. I didn't really mind, it sounded like they were having a lot of fun.

58

I said I was exhausted from all the Heaven to Tom, even though he promised there were more, even better parts, just over the horizon.

I wiped the tiredness out of my eyes at breakfast, and said, "I think I would rather just discuss our work, and we can make sure the lost souls don't get lost anymore, and maybe I can show you of soul binding, and you can show me of wing fitting."

Dominus was still grinning after our morning quickie, and I smiled at him. I showed *him* some new things, this time! Fantasies I always wished to do came to light in the morning dawn of Heaven, in our hotel, in our bed.

We finished breakfast and took the bus to Tom's office.

I waved good morning to Belladonna, who seemed strangely happy, and met the always happy woman called Holly! She greeted me with the biggest smile, and I think she one upped me in pleasantness! Holly said, "OHMYGOSH! You found an even *better* surprise for me, Tom!! A brand new friend!"

I smiled back at Holly, and said, "Yep! Tom found me alright, and said we'd be best friends right away!!"

Tom said, "...But I didn't-"

Holly said, "Oh, you Tom. You're the best boss I've ever had, I mean that. Lemme go show you what I do, Miss Lafaya Joliet Bonaparte!!"

Tom said, "...Boss?"

We ignored him, and Holly dragged me out the doors as Belladonna and Dominus talked about the shadier parts of life. Dominus seemed rather frustrated, as Holly dragged me out the doors, but Belladonna just put a hand on his shoulder and told him it would be ok.

We climbed a tree, and looked out on Heaven. It was a *really* big tree.

Holly just looked out at Heaven, and I whispered, "...What are we doing, Holly?"

She whispered back, "Shh. Just listen. I find this, and this found me."

I listened to the silence, up high in the tree, saw the clouds going past with angels flying over them, Heavenly structures all on top, with Heavenly nature surrounding. The wind blew past, and it was so very, very peaceful.

Holly said, "...Can you hear it?"

I said, "...I don't hear anything, just peaceful Heaven."

Holly said, "Exactly. That's my Father, God. He lets us have this beautiful, astounding peace, and you can hear him if you try hard enough. He found me, and took me under his wing. I grew up in that chapel, over there, under the best people I would be glad to call mother or father, but I know my Father is the Father of all of us."

"That's... very nice, Holly. I'm glad he found you a... good home. I wonder what it would've been like to even hit age 20, but I died pretty much as soon as I hit adulthood. I kinda still miss my parents..." I said.

Holly held my hand, and said, "You will see God can be a good dad too. If you want. I know you like Hell and all that, but if you ever want to hang out with me, or God, then that will be nice too."

"...Will I see Him, before I leave?" I said.

"I think so. He is already here, anyway, right beside us, always." Holly said.

We just… looked out on Heaven, and enjoyed the silence, under God's light.

Holly said, "Want me to fly you down??"

I perked up in happy surprise, and said, "Heaven yes!!"

Holly grabbed me under the armpits, over the chest, and we jumped out of the tree, her gliding and flapping through the air with me!! Our laughs carried through the peaceful silence.

59

Dominus was inspecting all the angel wings, and said, "This is astounding quality. Of course in Heaven they would only make something so beautiful... In Hell most demons have ratty, tattered wings, if they even have wings, and some can't even fly with them."

Joli watched as Belladonna made a wing, and said, "Hmm... I see... so this is sort of like accentuating the soul, with these wings, bringing out and harnessing the soul with these symbols of God..."

Huh. I never thought of it like that, but I suppose that is what it was...

Belladonna said, "At the start, Tom here couldn't make a baby's wings even if the baby was the least picky in all of Heaven, but he's grown a lot more at wing making, and is very resourceful when he sews."

Holly said, "I make sure we always have the right materials, especially, the most important part..."

Dominus said, "The feathers?"

"Nope! The string! Can't put a wing together if they're not connected right!" Holly said.

Joli said, "Oh! I notice the thread is so very fine, shimmers, and almost seems... to disappear, after a wing is made."

Belladonna handed me the classic angel wings, and I asked Dominus and Joli to watch me fit them.

The three eyed man looked nervous in my office, and said, "I-I spent so fuckin' long in Purgatory… but… Oh fuckin' God, are you going to stitch those into my body??"

I smiled kindly to Jake, the three eyed man, and said, "You won't feel a thing, just turn your back, and breathe calmly."

The man rubbed his scarless arms, and said, "I ain't a wimp to pain… I just thought, ever since my scars finally healed, making amendments for each one… That I wouldn't have to feel pain anymore. Alright. Just do it quick."

Jake shut his eyes, turned his back, and I said, "All done!"

Jake winked an eye open, looked at his back, and flapped his wings cautiously.

Joli said, "...That was it?"

Dominus said, "...Kind of quick. I expected something like the Queen's famed torturing."

Jake just jumped off the table, gasped, and said, "I-I feel s-so ligh'. I feel s-so fine. I gotta see Cass. Please lemme see my babe Cass."

I said, "She's waiting for you in the lobby, but first I have to give you somewhere to start in Heaven. You're a new soul, Jake, and I know you've lived a difficult life… You'll never have to do anything you had to do for work ever again. Executions aren't necessary, in Heaven, anyway, but you could still farm if you want, like you did later in life."

"Fuck tha'. I want a job that I don't have to watch a thousan' farmhands an' break my back workin' the scythe." Jake said.

"Hmm… Well, Cass has a restaurant, would you like to-" I said.

"Sign me up. I don't care what I do, as long as Cass is beside me, in her beautiful Heaven. Can I see… El-Elvis, too??" he said.

I shrugged, and said, "You can look for him, if that suits you. Well, you're all set. Enjoy your eternity, Jake."

I shook the man's hand firmly back, and he said, "Thank you, doc. I will. Now all you get outta my way, I gotta go hug my babe!!"

The man rushed to the lobby, and hugged Cass, the platinum blonde haired woman with pretty, sparkly, pink wings, close.

60

I taught Tom a bit about soul binding next. I said, "I was always pretty good in school, accepted all religions too, so I got accustomed to symbols."

Tom said, "Symbols?"

"Yes. A soul grasps onto many different things, little or big things, that can be summed up as symbols. A demon of gluttony could've seen herself as thin and anorexic before she became a demon of gluttony, so to bind her soul back together I find the parts of her that she loved about herself, before the self hate consumed her mind and body. I found the symbol of her soul." I said.

"So... like a rattle, or a toy? Something for when the soul was pure?" Tom said.

"Sometimes. But for this demon I had to find that symbol that was beside her in life, before she gorged herself to death. It turned out to be a coffee mug. I found all the pieces of this little mug, scattered around a restaurant and even stolen by other demons, reattached them... then wham! I slammed it with my blacksmith's hammer." I said.

"...Seems counterproductive, for all the time spent to rebuild the soul..." Tom said.

"Oh, no! When I hit souls right with my blacksmith's hammer, a gift to me from the Queen of Hell, the soul comes back together from pieces. I then filled the mug with coffee, and me and her had a nice coffee break. She laughed and smiled, saying she got the mug as a birthday present, before everything got so awful for her, and... as soon as she finished the coffee, she was human again! Exactly how she wanted to look, not too fat, not too skinny." I said.

Tom said, "...Interesting. I like that you and her made an act to seal this soul, at the end, an acceptance of her soul so to speak."

We did? Oh! I guess we did.

Tom said, "I urge you to keep doing what you're doing, Joli. People *need* to have the chance to realize they are worth more, whether that be through the acceptance of God or only themself, your soul is a remarkable and beautiful thing, never to be forsaken. I imagine you must be quite popular in the underworld, giving all those demons second chances."

I laughed, and said, "Hardly! I make a lot of enemies with the *very* evil demons... Beelzebub is still pissed at me for interrupting his restaurant whilst looking for the soul I mentioned from earlier, and others... Well, if I didn't have the Queen on my side, I'm sure I'd be chopped up, burned, tortured, flayed, disembowled, thrown off a cliff, fed to demons, raped, murdered, lacerated, and so much more! Over and over again, too!"

Tom laughed, and said, "Well... Ok. Stay safe. I'll call Max and let him know you're ready to go. He said it's no trouble at all."

I said, "...But what about the missing souls? We have so much work to do in finding them!"

"The herald angel said for us both to keep doing our jobs, and those souls, and the reason for their disappearance, will surface in time. I think that's a good plan of action." Tom said.

"...And... I'm afraid to ask, but... I really... really... wanted to meet... my grandma. And God, if that's not too much trouble." I said.

Tom looked at me surprised, and said, "We should've done that right away! That God can be a tricky one to track down, at times… But your grandma is probably eager as a beaver to see you again."

"I… kinda… didn't want to disappoint her, now that I'm dead… I'm sure she must think I got into all sorts of trouble! But I miss her." I said.

Tom smiled kindly, and said, "Let's go and meet her. Let me check my files, to see where she might be located."

Tom took out a huuuuuge book, opened it up, after blowing off the dust on it, and found my grandma's address.

61

Joli was so nervous, as we took the bus, gripping onto Dominus's hand as if her life depended on it. We got to an apartment complex, and Joli said, "Is that an old person's home?? Oh god, please don't let it be an old person's home."

I shook my head, and we got off the bus.

We got to apartment number 777, and I knocked on the door. We heard loud music playing from inside, and someone from inside said, "One sec, guys! Probably another for the party!"

A smiling, young woman, around Joli's age, opened the door, smiling friendly to us.

Joli gasped, and said, "G-G-Grandma??"

The young woman gasped louder, and said, "My darling Lafaya!! Ohmygosh, let me hug you, my sweet."

The young woman hugged Joli, and for a second... I saw an old woman hugging her granddaughter close, the granddaughter crying against her shoulder.

The image faded, and the young woman said, "And who are these two, my Lafaya? Heya babes, care to come inside?"

Joli nodded, and we walked into a party of Heaven. In surprise, I noticed they were playing songs by... me. I never, *ever* recorded these songs. Never got a chance to.

Joli explained that Dominus was her boyfriend, and I was a wing fitter showing her Heaven.

The woman… who I guess we just called Grandma, said, "Good. That's what a wing fitter is supposed to do for new angels. We're going to have so much fun, Lafaya! I gotta show you all to my friends! That's Pepper, Jace, Nicky, Basil-"

Joli carefully explained, "I won't be staying, Grandma."

Grandma said, "...What do you mean, Lafaya? I always like spending time with my favorite, and only, granddaughter!"

Joli smiled sadly, and said, "I live in Hell, Grandma. I work there as a soul binder, binding souls together from pieces. I-I- I wish I could stay."

Grandma said, "B-But you can! Nothing is stopping you! Y-You need to stay here, be safe. Lafaya, I forbid you from going back to that dangerous place! I learned about those poor missing souls, and I can't bear to think my Lafaya is going to be one of them!"

Joli just continued to smile sadly, and said, "I'm sorry, Grandma, but it is my choice. I will… definitely come to visit, a lot, and I am so very happy to see you again. Having you die when I was a kid was very difficult for me."

Grandma said, "But you're still a kid! You shouldn't have- have-died so young! Oh… Come here, my darling Lafaya…"

Grandma and Joli hugged each other close on the couch, as the party was silent, as my music still played.

Joli spent a good while reconnecting with her grandma, Grandma meeting Dominus and I, who Grandma flirted with us slightly and politely, and then we left the apartment, waving goodbye to everyone. I had an intense discussion with Basil about my music, and I never knew I had fans so far, even in the afterlife, and even if they were medieval knights from old England.

Max waited on the curb, in the pale car, and I hugged Joli close, and gave Dominus a firm handshake. I bid them safety, and they got in the back of the car. Joli said to me, "D-Do you think we'll see eachother again?"

I saw someone approach from the street, the herald angel, walking down the road and smoking a pipe, and I said to her, "I'm sure in no time. See you soon, Joli."

I stepped back, waved them goodbye, and Max drove the two back down to Hell.

5

The Pure Souls

Hark, the herald angel approacheth. How ya doing?

62

"Hi, herald. I'm well, how are you?" I said.

"Well, I've been absolutely wonderful!! Turning off the bold voice, cuz I just gotta guy out with you, my man!! My two lovely ladies..." the herald angel then sighed, in love, "Are going to be helping us in this next quest!! I love a good quest, and I love it when Yule and Jane can kick ass and take names!!" he said.

"...I kinda envy you, dude. Two lovely ladies, and I've got a living wife..." I said, as we walked down the night street of Heaven. I started a cigarette as he continued to smoke his pipe.

"I wouldn't be envious, you've got that good love, and a promise of it, for the rest of your eternity... I mean, I do too, but my gals are very relaxed. It took a long time to start this relationship with them, and I am so thankful for it, every day." he said.

"...But what if my wife-" I said.

He said, "Do you remember her promise to you, too?"

I thought back, and I said, "...Yeah. That she'd always be with me, on our wedding day."

"Exactly. Lucky for you, the promise turned out to be true. I mean, she can always find a nice trophy husband in time, but I'm sure it would just be for fun." he said.

I rolled my eyes, and we got to the gas station.

I waved hello to my rainbow winged friend, the cashier, and we got some snack cakes, sandwiches, chips, soda, and beer, the herald angel piled the stuff into his backpack, and I carried the beer.

"...So what is this 'quest' you mentioned?" I asked.

"...Isn't it obvious by now? We're going to the living world to inspect the disappearance of the pure souls! Gotta be something fishy, like old dwellers from before time, mhm, gotta be old dwellers." he said.

I said, as we left the gas station and I waved goodbye to the cashier, "...There's such a thing as old dwellers?"

He said, "Gotta be, right? Only thing that makes sense that would be able to mess up the rules! ...I'm probably just too much of an H.P. Lovecraft fan, to be honest..."

I blinked, as the herald angel started *another* smoke on his pipe, and we got to his dark grey, dented, 2000 camry parked in an empty lot.

The herald angel popped the trunk, and I threw the beer in the back, fleetingly noticing Jane and Yule making out in the back of his car. They smiled and giggled, waving at me. I waved back, and smiled.

I got in the passenger seat, as the herald angel started the car. I greeted the ladies and they shook my hand politely. Jane gave me a little wink, and Yule... looked intense, excited, and like she could take on the world.

We drove down the road, the herald angel blasting the music, and St. Peter opened the gates for us, Yule and Jane blowing him kisses as he did. St. Peter caught a few kisses, and put them to his heart close.

We drove down some empty clouds outside of Heaven, and the herald angel said, "So this cloud, this one here, right, Yule?"

"Yep. Just drive off it as fast as you can, and scream as much as you like! That's what I did when I first went to the living world." Yule said.

"Wait, what...?" I said.

The herald angel slammed on the gas, and we drove off the cloud, going straight... down.

We screamed as we saw... *the Earth...* approach from beneath us.

63

I sighed, looking out the castle windows... Max dropped us off, and Hana wished to meet me. I threw all the stuff from Heaven in my closet, except for the everliving flowers put in a vase, and... the shirt given to me by my grandma. I put that on, and went to visit her majesty.

Hana was sitting in the throne room, taking complaints and grievances from demons all through Hell. She looked tired, but also very relaxed. Sara had left before I got back, and you could see that gentle chill in Hana's body called postcoitus bliss.

Hana said to a demon, "Oh? You want *more* books? What have you been doing with all of them?"

"Well, Marbas, the demon of knowledge, told us how to consume the power of the books!" the demon said.

"...And that would be?" Hana said.

"Eating them, oh Queen! They do taste a little funny, but I feel smarter already!" the demon said.

"...How about we get you all to a proper school, run by demons of *proper* knowledge, and you can learn how to read. Marbas does like his little pranks, doesn't he..." Hana said.

The demon's smile left, and he said, *"...But I thought Moby Dick was the tastiest out of all of them... Ok. Thank you, my liege. Your everflowing kindness shall drown and destroy Hell in the happiest ocean. May we suffer through your enlightened reign for all eternity and longer, and-"*

Hana waved her hand, and said, "Yes, yes, all that. Next!"

Beleth noticed me, and whispered in Hana's ear.

Hana perked up a smile, and said, "Joli! Come, let me feel you! I bet you've got a big smile on your face, from being in Heaven!"

I went up to her, let her feel my face, and Hana frowned, saying, "What's with the frown, Joli?"

"I… I don't know. I thought I'd be happy, too. But I feel strangely sad for what I gave up." I said.

Hana said, "You always have the power to leave, anytime you wish. You are not chained to me, and always belong to God."

I sighed, and said, "Thank you, Hana. I'd like to save a soul before bed, if that's ok-"

A demon, a tall, crooked standing demon walked past the line to Hana, and shouted, *"So you are the soul 'bender.' You have twisted my wife's soul, corrupting and deceiving her with malice. You should be ashamed. She left for Purgatory, like THAT will make her less of a stupid bitch..."*

I stood tall against this demon, and said, "Oh. I remember you. You are the one slave master who even enslaved his wife. She desired freedom, and I gave her a chance to have that, her own way-"

"You corrupt and destroy good, powerful demons. You make us lose our way. I ought to whip you until you fall before me, filthy wench-" the demon said.

Hana boomed, *"And if you do, I will...* Hm. What have I not tried yet, Beleth?" Beleth whispered in her ear, and she said, "Ah! Yes, that'll do. Roll that thing out here and let's have some fun, everyone!"

The demon paled, as the other demons cheered, and Hana's servants went to the dungeon to get… something… so I quickly said, "Allow me a chance to prove this demon wrong, Hana. Allow me to bind his soul together."

"Aww... Really? I keep forgetting we have that thing! Ok, servants, cancel the order, let's watch a soul binder work. All yours, Joli." Hana said.

I smiled, and the demon stood crooked and defiant against me again.

64

...Strangely... we slowed in our descent, and landed gently, peacefully, tires softly touching the road.

The herald angel opened his eyes, as Yule and Jane whooped in delight, and the herald angel screeched the wheels and took off racing down the road.

Jane sighed looking out the window, and said, “Been a long time since we've been here, eh, guys?”

The herald angel said, “Yeah. Almost too long. I could cruise down this highway for all time...”

Yule said, “Well, 'nuff o' that! We gotta go to the first disappearance, a good soul who died, a little, pure baby... It's very sad, but what's sadder is that this baby isn't in Heaven!! It makes me terrified for him! Our angels of death have been searching nonstop for this soul, but I think we may find something at-”

Jane said, “We're not going to look at dead babies, are we? That seems a little unnecessary.”

“...No! I didn't mean doing *that...* The baby has been cremated and buried already, so we're going to make an inspection with the mother and father. Just up the road, here!!” Yule said.

The herald angel drove into a suburban town, and I looked gently out the window at life pass by. It all seemed... so foreign, now. The streets seemed drabby, the dark clouds so grey, the houses shabby, the trash blew by in the wind, and-

The herald angel said, "Ahh… I love this sight, don't you, Tom? That pure, bleak feeling known only as life… I'm glad this town is kinda run down, I couldn't stand going somewhere like I grew up."

I said, "...Where was that, again?"

"Basically suburbia! These two ladies lived in far different places, Jane grew up in Hell, and Yule grew up in old, old Germany, from when they were only tribes! I'm just a no good American, and fuckin' small towns, man…" the herald angel said, shaking his head.

I shrugged at this.

It started raining, as the thunder already had been premonitioning this. Up above the clouds everything looked so peaceful, stars twinkling down on life… but down below, the gloominess of life was ever present.

We parked near a house, and heard shouting and yelling coming from inside, then a man barged out, and the woman from the door said, "Don't *ever* come back!! Our baby was the only thing keeping us together, so go… *fuck yourself!!*"

"That'd be better than fucking you, you goddamned cunt!!" the man yelled back as he walked away, and she slammed the door.

He went to the bus stop, and we followed him slightly.

He stood there, looking angry, smoking a cigarette… then cried and screamed in frustration, in anger, and I felt pity for this man in the rain.

And then he prayed. We could hear him, despite the constant drizzle of the rain.

He said, "God. Take me away now." and that was all.

The herald angel said, "Looks like we've been called, everyone!"

I protested, but the herald angel parked in front of the man, and Yule opened up the door for him.

The man looked at us quizzically, but shrugged and got in the backseat with the ladies.

"Thanks." he said, "It's been storming so awfully these days."

As I realized this man in the rain could hear, feel, and see us, the herald angel said, "Where you going, man?"

"I don't know… Could you just drop me off in town? I know a few guys at the pub who might take me in. My… girlfriend and I broke up." he said.

"A shame." the herald angel said, "We were just going to get drinks, and would like a dry patch to wet our whistles."

The man smiled gently, and said, "I'll give you directions. Thanks."

We drove down the road, and parked at the pub, getting wet from the rain and then going into the pub.

65

The crooked demon was malicious, evil, and did not want my help. I helped him anyway.

I tried to single out the point that he became bad, but he seemed to always have been bad, according to Hana! She said he was the perfect soul for Hell, grew up cruel and privileged, became a wrathful slave master, seduced his way into a woman's arms, even killed her past husband, and lived to old age, as a miser. He seemed to have lived a blessed life, but all that was before me was an angry, spiteful demon.

Hana said a nice torture will help him change his attitude far over trying to save his soul, and I could tell the demon knew it wouldn't be a simple slap on the wrist. Whenever he looked at Hana, he would tremble, even though Hana just looked into the blind distance with a pleasant smile.

I hmmed, and asked Hana how his torture would be different than a normal racking or something.

Hana said, "Oh! I love talking about this stuff, even though I always freak people out! Well, I'd first *love* to deprive him of anything but shadow and hunger, just to brainwash him a bit and have him lose his marbles, then I'd *like,* even though it's not *always* necessary, to torment him with everything he's ever loved, which for him happens to be cruelty. Then I'd bring the thing out, and then we'd watch… him! I'd like to see how he fares against that… thing!"

The crooked demon begged, *"Isn't there a better way… than that thing?? I could work for you, oh Queen, I'd be a dedicated slaveholder and master-"*

I said, "She needs no masters nor slaveholders. Your wife hated everything about you, and only seemed to have gone to Hell because she was still chained to you in the afterlife, and helped you in your evil in the end. You will never see her ever again, demon."

The crooked demon sneered at me.

I said, "Oh, I'm hungry. I think I'd like a snack, you can start the torture if you like, Hana, but I think I'll enjoy my southern style chicken and work more on him tomorrow…"

The crooked demon whimpered, *"Y-You have southern style chicken??"*

I said, "Oh yes, the best. I'll throw you the bones."

Hana clapped her hands together in a smile, and said, "Deprive him! Oh yes, deprive my subject of even me! Go on, Beleth. Tear up his soul a bit, but make sure you know where the pieces are."

Beleth smiled wickedly, and could not get any words out but mad cackling.

Beleth put the crooked demon in chains, and whispered something in his ear.

The crooked demon questioned Beleth, *"Music is in my ear? What do you mean?"*

Beleth whispered, *"That will be our phrase, my darling, so you know whenever you hear my whispering, you are listening to eternal music…"*

Beleth cackled, and kicked the crooked demon down the stairs to the dungeon.

The rest of the demons filed out, congratulating Hana on some well done sovereigning.

Hana looked dreamily at the ceiling, and said, "Ahh… The ol' 'music is in my ear' trick… So pleasant. Well! Good night, Joli. I'm gonna go call Sara and hit the hay too. I'm so excited to see how our prisoner will be shredded tomorrow! Gonna be a blast."

I sighed, feeling like I failed, and got my snack and went to my room where Dominus was hanging out, reading from a few books from Heaven.

He said, "I never knew there could *also* be such a lust, a lust for good books. The tantalizing sensory descriptions… If only I could touch them, but that makes them just so much more tantalizing…"

I asked him, "How come it was so easy to bind your soul together? How come you're not like… like Hana's new prisoner?"

He said, "Hm? Oh, did our Queen catch a live one? I think it had something to do with you genuinely caring for me, and me caring back. Can't save some guy's soul if you don't care."

I said, "Oh… I guess I should figure out how to relate with that guy, even though I absolutely *hated* the stories his wife told me… Well. Wanna fuck?"

Dominus said, "One second, Joli, I just have to finish this part, this one part here."

I shrugged, went to bed, realized that 'this one part' encompassed the entire rest of the book, and went to sleep.

66

We drank at the pub, the herald with his two ladies in his arms. The man in the rain in the pub whispered to me, and said, "...I thought the cute one was with you?"

I said, "Oh, no. I'm married. They're just friends of mine."

"...Lucky fucker. I'd take that cute one and drive off to the sunset in a happy ending... but I really am thankful to you guys. Hard to meet someone so nice these days. Most would simply drive past, and even laugh at it." he said.

I wondered which one of the ladies was 'the cute one.' I think something else drove the herald's relationship with these women, than simply being with a cute face. The women also loved each other just as much as him, and seemed to really be the cool cats in the pub. The three would laugh and joke, the herald getting in intense one on one discussions with everyone, despite being so friendly, Yule would challenge any man or woman to games of skill or strength, and in general just made you feel safe and at ease, and Jane would pull out the best jokes, but never at someone's expense.

I sipped at my drink, as the ladies were talking to some other cool ladies, and saw the intense, serious stare given to me by the herald angel.

I realized this was work, and not fun.

I tried to grill the man in the rain in the pub about his relationship with his girlfriend, trying to bring out the subject of the death of his son. The man didn't seem to want to talk about it, and would get very frustrated whenever I did talk about his girlfriend.

I said, "Well, that's a big point of why you're here, right?"

He said, "I know, I just... I lost a kid a while back, and it's just hard to talk about."

Jackpot. I said, "Let's get some more booze, and forget about it for now."

He accepted, but said, "But I don't want to forget about Jerome. He was... my little baby. I was going to teach him baseball, what trading cards are worth, dad things."

We got some whiskey, and the man continued.

He said, "I was going to show him how to pick up chicks, who knows if he'd be any good at it, like I am. As soon as he became an adult I was going to drink him under the table..."

I said, "At least he's in a better place."

He said, "And where's that?"

I said I didn't know.

"Then keep your religious sentiment to yourself. My son is dead. And there's nothing anyone can do to bring him back." he said.

We sipped on the whiskey in silence, and the man found another drinker like him to crash on their couch for a while.

I felt like... I felt like I failed. There was a lost soul, somewhere in the afterlife, and these people's lives would never be the same because the soul was dead and gone.

I sighed, wishing the man in the rain in the pub goodnight, and was going to follow the herald angel, the seraph, and the angel of Hell out the door, and the man clasped my shoulder, and said, "Thanks, Tom. I don't think I'll ever forget this kindness, even though it doesn't seem like much. Tell your wife hi for me, and tell that lucky sonofabitch to treat his ladies well."

The herald angel winked at the man, the man rolled his eyes, and I went to the car in the rain with the trio.

67

I woke up in the morning, passed the throne room and said hello to Hana on her throne-

Wait. That wasn't Hana. She was skinnier, taller, looked so much like her, and was watching me with intense, watchful eyes.

I stuttered, "Wh-What are y-you doing on Hana's throne? That place is meant only for the Queen." I tried to keep composure, but I could not get past my fear of those eyes, which seemed to be looking to my very soul.

She said, "Ah yes... I thought I was taking only a brief vacation, but it seems things have changed drastically since I've been gone... My daughter seems to have taken on my goals for her... Very well. I bequeath my rights as Queen of Hell completely to my daughter. You are my witness, strange little girl."

I gasped, and recognized her from the statue I saw. I said, "You're Miss Dina, the old Queen of Hell."

She got off the throne, bowed to me, and said, "That I am. How is my daughter? And *what* is some human doing in Hell that is not her?"

"I-I'm Joli, I came here as a lost soul, but work under Hana as a soul binder now." I said.

"Soul binder? And *lost* souls? This in fact would be the perfect time to launch an invasion on Heaven and creation, with the afterlife somehow not being stable... but no matter, it is out of my hands. Where is my daughter? Wasting time with her friends again?" Dina said.

"Sh-She could be in the dungeon, roughing up her new prisoner. I'm going there to try and bind his soul together, would you care to join me?" I asked.

"Of course, Lafaya Joliet Bonaparte. Lead the way." Dina said.

I had not told her my full name. What else did this woman know of me that she could see without it being visible?

We walked down the dark, gloomy steps, past dark, gloomy empty cells, to the torture chamber.

Dina said, as we passed the cells, "I was once imprisoned in a cell just like this, in a Hell that was rebellious and destructive. I would've filled these cells with all sorts of scum, but it seems Hana is a bit more lenient."

"You lived in this castle before, right?" I asked.

"Never would I dream of such a dismal abode. I lived a normal life in a normal house in Hell, as a normal all powerful Queen of the Underworld. I think Hana grew up on too many fantasy stories in her youth..." Dina said.

Before we got to the torture chamber, I had to ask Dina, "What *are* you doing here??"

Dina smiled, and said, "I wish to see something I haven't seen in a long time. I wish to see my daughter's smile."

We got to the torture chamber lit by torches, and saw Hana smiling, ripping and tearing at the demon with her knife. She said to the crooked demon, "Not so crooked now, are we? How's it feel to *see what I see??*"

The demon whimpered, only pieces, as Beleth laughed and laughed in the corner.

But Hana wiped off her bloody hands, and said, "I... I feel something... I feel someone. *Mom??*"

Dina hugged her daughter, and said, "So nice to see you enjoying the work, dear. I love you."

Hana burst out smiling and crying at the same time, hugged Dina back, and said, "I love you too, Mom."

68

We parked in an empty lot and slept in the car, the herald angel in the back with Yule and Jane, and I fell asleep in the passenger seat, uncomfortable but cozy, listening to the rain pitter patter on the car...

I woke up to dazzling sunlight with a crick in my neck, and saw the three sitting outside drinking beer and eating our supplies next to a small fire Jane had started.

They were talking about a strange subject, as I got out of the car. Jane said, "...so yeah, I always wanted to rape my rapist."

Yule said, "I don't think I could ever forgive one for doing so to me, but I also don't think you could safely rape your rapist and not have it unwind into more terror."

The herald angel said, "That sort of thing is just a downward spiral, and always seems to get you hurt, Jane."

Jane said, "I know. That's why we roleplay it out, you and I, instead of me actually hunting someone down and forcing them to submit... It feels safe, comfortable, and I know we can do whatever we like during."

I said, "Er, good morning, guys."

The herald angel said, "Morning, Tom. So, tell us what you learned from the poor father. We've got some sandwiches we're warming up, too."

I sat beside them by the fire, and Jane passed me a toasty Heaven sandwich and Yule passed me a beer, and I said, "Seems like he has a lot of regret regarding the death of his son. Was he just not religious enough for the baby to find its way to Heaven? Was the baby just not baptized or something?"

Yule said, "I don't think so. The pure souls are *pure.* Even if some of them aren't baptized, they sure never belong in Hell."

Jane said, "...Neither did I... Could the current ruler of Hell be doing something shady we don't know about?"

I said, "Nah, Hanatrix is the most upstanding Queen of Hell I've ever seen, but I've never seen a Queen of Hell before."

The herald angel said, "So, Jane and I are going to make a few rounds looking for the other souls, and Yule will go with you to see if you can warm up to the girlfriend to learn information about the dead son. I checked what she does on a daily schedule, and if she's not too frustrated and flustered from the changes in her life, she should be going to the park to take her morning walk, soon..."

I said, "It seems kind of weird hunting her down. Like we're stalking her or something."

Yule said, "We're angels, Tom. We're always listening, and always watching. We'll leave her her privacy if she asks, but if we can help a grieving soul find peace, then we should."

I agreed, saying, "Alright. Let's check out the park, then."

Jane and the herald angel drove off down the road, and Yule took my arm in hers and we strolled down the street. We made small talk, enjoying each other's stride, and she said, "Yep! My lovers sure are great, aren't they? I'm the one who got them into the whole multiple loves thing, and since we all knew each other for so long beforehand, it just came easy!"

"...Isn't that kind of a gamble, though? How can you maintain the equality with each of them?" I asked.

"That's the thing! Love ain't equal! We always love our lovers in different, astounding ways. Trying to compare them to each other... It's just impossible! Jane is like, a little sister in a different way to me, in a much more intimate way. And my lovely herald... I can call him the writer of my life, and be happy with it." Yule said.

"...That's... cool. I actually think that's something very unique, that your relationship works. But how do you-" I said.

"Shh. We'll talk about *that* later. There's our quarry, crying by the pond." Yule said.

69

I asked Hana, "...This isn't the part where you heal him from pieces to torture him more, is it?"

Hana stopped hugging her mom, and said to me, "Oh, nah. I actually thought if we broke him down a bit it would make *your* job easier, Joli. Would you care to inspect this soul to see what we should do, Mom? We're trying to save his soul. You may have some hidden insight for us."

Dina said, "Oh, no. I think I'd prefer to sit with Beleth and watch, if that is ok. How are you, Beleth my dear? Haven't decided to betray my daughter and name yourself supreme overlord of all creation yet, I see."

Beleth gasped for breath after laughing so long, and said, *"Oh... OH! Hana! You're so cruelly humorous when you're really working the blade! No, Miss Dina, I have been enjoying this time, even though that end goal is always beckoning me forward..."*

I said, "B-But I thought you said you were loyal to H-Hana, Beleth."

Hana said, "Oh, we all know Beleth is a treacherous piece of scum. That's why I like him! Even as I was a young girl he would try to sew blasphemous evil into my fertile mind... Really learned a lot from him, I sure did, even though there are far better flute teachers than a demon of music..."

Beleth smiled, and said, *"And yet still, my lessons for you on music ring true. You can even make others sing with far more useful instruments."*

"E flat." Hana said, and nicked the tortured demon with her blade.

The demon whimpered in E flat. Beleth burst out laughing in delight.

Hana said, "Here are his pieces, Joli. Try to construct them into something a little more respectful, this time. *No one* threatens the Queen's friends."

Hana handed me a big bag of red, and I realized Hana *did* do this to defend me as well as herself... but was this really necessary?

I asked Hana this, and she said, "No, not really. But when in Rome... or Hell, do what the demons do. If you would one day gather respect for your own customs, you must not wholly discard others'. This is what demons like, so this is what demons get."

The now straight tortured demon whimpered, *"My Queen... please, allow me to serve you... I wish... to make amends, for my foolishness..."*

Hana said, "See?"

I looked at her quizzically, and went to the tortured demon and gently held his hand. I said, "You do not need to suffer anymore-"

He ripped his hand away from mine, and said, *"I only... will... serve the Queen... Do not touch me, you FILTH..."*

I stepped back, disgusted.

Here was a creature that was destroyed by his liege, and yet still, would serve her for an endless more amount of torture.

I got really angry at this, and shouted and screamed at the demon, telling him I was here to help him, to put him back together, to bind his soul into what he always wanted.

Yet still, he said, *"I only want to serve the Queen."*

I was flabbergasted, and Dina gently held my hand, and said, "We should let this man rest, if you would like to help him. Take his pieces and see if you can reverse them into a primal form of soul, and maybe you can figure out how to help the whole."

I looked at Dina who looked kindly back at me, and Dina, Hana, and I left the torture chamber.

Beleth said, *"Music is in my ear."* as soon as he and the prisoner were alone again.

70

Yule got a call from her prayer phone, and answered a crying woman's call. I let her talk, and asked the other crying woman if she was ok, the woman whose baby we were supposed to find.

She sniffled, and said, "P-Please leave me alone... I don't want to talk about it."

I knew sometimes when people don't want to talk about something, especially if they're crying in agony, sometimes they really do.

I gently sat beside her, as she continued to cry into her hands, and said, "I'm Tom. I'm sorry for what happened."

She said, "Oh... So you're someone from church? I hate how everyone knows my baby is dead... It's none of their business..."

"Yes, I know. But we all care for you, every one of us. It's a tragedy, and can never be rectified-" I said.

"No. It can't. I'm alone. Even my *bastard* boyfriend left me, and I don't know what to do..." she said, and looked into my eyes while crying.

I gently said, "God will watch over you. I just wanted to tell you that everyone cares, and you're not alone."

"Thank you. I was going to teach my baby how to be a gentleman, how to treat the ladies nice and even teach him how to cook well... Make brownies and cakes with him, and then we could watch movies, laughing in delight... Now... there's only his silence, forever..." she said.

I said, "I think if you listen closely to that silence, you'll find there's really so much going on. Care to join me?"

She sniffled and nodded, and we listened to the wind go past, the sound of geese on the pond, the cars going past in the distance, people talking far away, and-

I heard a baby's laughter.

The crying woman smiled, and said, "It's like I can hear Jerome, as we played with him, in the peace around us. Thank you, mister. I'm-"

I quickly said, "I'm sorry, but I have to go. Take care, now!"

I waved Yule with me, and we ran down the path, to where I heard the baby laughing.

We looked at a spot, a patch of nature, and I said, "This is where I heard the pure soul, Yule, this is the spot."

Yule inspected the ground, the surroundings, and said, "No use, Tom. The soul seems to have moved on."

"Then that means the soul is... in Hell?" I asked.

"I don't know. Let's go back to the others, and see what they found. The call I got was from my friend Nevaeh, who just feels terrible about setting this couple up and having everything get ruined, even their baby's soul being lost..." Yule said.

"It's not her fault, and we're here to fix things." I said.

Yule nodded, and we walked back to the empty lot.

71

Hana picked up the baby that was crying on the throne room floor.

Hana said, as she held the baby close, "Is this what I think it is?"

Dina said, "I think your problem just got a little worse, sweetheart. Even the most innocent pure souls are landing in your domain.

The baby cried, hungry, and Hana stuttered, "Wh-What am I supposed to do with a *baby??* Joli here was one thing, but a *baby...*"

Dina shrugged, and said, "I'll go see if we can't find any formula for him. Kitchen is this way, correct?"

Hana said, "Just through the arches with the stone jutting out. And how the fuck is it a him?? Babies are all amalgamous blobs until a certain age, anyway!!"

The baby just laughed in Hana's arms.

I blinked at the baby, and I started smiling. I think such a cute little guy was giving me back my spirit! I felt so depressed and angry, unable to bind that wicked soul, and I asked Hana if I could hold him!

She said, handing the baby to me, "All yours, man. I name you an official baby caretaker-"

The baby started crying in my arms, and I said, "Oops! I think he likes you. Here you go." and gave Hana back the baby who became quiet in her arms.

Hana sighed, and Dina came back with a bottle filled with mixture.

Hana sat on her throne and fed the baby with the bottle, and Dina smiled and said, "This is adorable. I always wanted you to have children, Hana, but your lifestyle never particularly allowed for one..."

Hana said, "I couldn't be a mother! I was a teacher to half the kids in Lux's school! All those snot nosed brats... I couldn't bear having to really make the commitment to a kid, and end up ruining him somehow..."

Dina politely said, "I mean that you're a lesbian, Hana."

Hana blushed a little bit, and said, "...Yeah, so?"

Dina said, "Well, when a man and a woman love each other very much... and not when a woman and a woman do... You get the picture."

Hana said, "Ha. Ha. Cut the jokes, Mom, and please help Joli do something with that damned slaveholder... I gotta get him outta here, having a guy like that near a baby is no good!"

Dominus came down from my room, walking and reading, carefully avoiding walls as he was, and then he heard the baby burp.

Dominus ran down the steps, and awwed at Hana's baby.

He said, "I can't wait to meet my descendents. I know I probably have a few, somewhere. This guy is so cute, Hana!"

Oh yeah. Sex leads to babies, and Dominus had a lot of sex...

I ignored the fact of how many descendents Dominus had, probably just like him that I had to introduce myself to eventually. I just sat with Dina at the table, pouring out the bag of red. Dominus oohed and played with the baby in Hana's arms, as Hana looked annoyed.

Dina looked closely at a bit of the demon, and said, "It definitely looks like demonic cells in his body, not a pure cell amongst them... Even has bacteria of the soul clung to each chunk..."

"How can you see that?? Are your eyes microscopes?" I asked her.

Dina smiled, and said, "While my daughter can see in other ways, I can see all in all ways."

I paused at this, and said, "...What if we tried to make a cure for the cells? That'd work, right? Something soul worthy..."

Dina shrugged, and said, "You could try. I think throwing all the bits to the demon to him and then rekilling him could allow him to recombobulate together, and he may thank you for that. If you made this cure for this soul bacteria, you could infect him with the cure without him knowing at the start…"

"Ooh. Devious. Do the cells in any way show a distinct sign of deterioration? I'm guessing at the time they multiply." I said.

Dina said, "Why yes, they do. That is the distinct point of the demon's recorruption."

"Perfect. This demon is just stuck in his ways, and we have to find him a new path…" I said.

Hana told the baby sweetly, "Please shut up, I can't take such cute little laughter. *It hurts my ears."*

The baby continued to laugh, as Hana sighed.

72

Jane was smoking and in an intense discussion with the herald angel, sitting on the car. I heard her say, "It's gotta be Satan. No way it's not Satan, and-"

The herald angel said, "I think there is so much more evil than just that particular figure. It could just be a mistake, as well."

"Well, as leader of this convoy, I choose to-" Jane said.

Yule said as we approached, "Who made you leader, Jane? I vote Tom chooses what to do next. He found a trail of a pure soul."

The herald angel said, "Really? Jane and I have been hitting dead ends all through town. Just disappearances of souls, without a distinct trace at all… Ok. Tom, I vote you choose."

Jane said, "...I still think we should go to Hell, and kick Satan's ass, *one more time...*"

I said, "Actually, I agree to go to Hell, Jane. These souls are being taken there, and if we can find what is attracting them, then we should fix the problem."

Yule and the herald angel sighed, and Jane said, "Yessss. I can't wait to finally *kill him.* I know I can, I just have to figure out how…"

I opened my eyes in surprise, and said, "You can kill the Devil?"

Yule sighed angrily again, and said, "No, you can't. You can't destroy a soul, but that's what Satan has been trying to do for all his creation. The best solution we've found to destroy someone so evil is to lock him up, in Hell, with no way out..."

Jane said, "And he escapes, over and over. We just need to chop him up and burn him, this time, then send him to space, far away."

The herald angel shook his head, and said, "We're getting off topic... but if we did that, someone else'd just be stuck with our problems. Let's get going, and say goodbye to rundown suburbia."

We got in the car, Jane up front and Yule and I in the back.

Jane gave directions to the portal of Hell.

I guess that's where she escaped to the living world in the first place, and then made the transition from demon, to human, to angel.

We got to the highway, and drove a long time.

We got to a park, and walked down the trail.

We got to a dead tree, with nothing around it growing.

Jane said, "Here we are. Let me see... Oh. I don't know, someone kick it or something."

The herald angel kicked the dead tree, and a chunk fell off, leading to a dark portal to Hell.

They walked into that darkness, and left me outside, unsure of what to do.

I looked into that horrible darkness, gulped, said a prayer for luck, and charged in after them.

Yule and Jane lit their flames to guide the way, and we walked down the dark, dismal stairs to the underworld.

We kept walking, endlessly.

Each step felt heavy to me, even though we were going downwards. It was so steep.

I thought we'd spend eternity just walking down to Hell, but we soon got to a dark black river.

Jane said, "Ahh... My horror returns to me. How pleasant. There's the ferry, with my ol' pal Charon."

A dark, hooded figure rowed a ferry to us, and said, *"Welcome back, Jane. I guess I should quit my complaining this time and just give you the ride, eh?"*

Jane said, "Right on, Charon. And I expect no funny business. You're never getting into these knickers, so get used to it."

Charon said, *"I told you you'd break something, if you got out... You broke my heart. Ok, that's fine. Hello, all. Enjoy the trip to Hell."*

We got on the ferry, and Charon rowed us over the river.

There, snarling and waiting for us on the bank, was a three headed dog... Cerberus.

Jane scowled at Charon, and said, "Get some extra security, did we?"

Charon grinned, and said, *"Good luck, Mary Jane."* and rowed back over the river.

73

I put southern style chicken in the demon bits bag, threw the bag to the tortured demon, and said to Beleth, "Ok. Kill him now."

Beleth frowned at me, and said, *"Music is in my ears?"*

The tortured demon moaned, *"MUSIC IS IN MY EARS!!"*

I watched as Dina went up to the tortured demon, saying, "I'll do it. I'll make sure he's completely and totally dead."

She looked at the demon, I blinked, the demon was turned to ash, I blinked again, and the demon was reformed, gasping for breath.

He then felt his stomach, and said, *"I feel... well, besides the horrible torture... I feel... full... and that ma'velous aftertaste..."*

I said, "I fed you southern style chicken. Hope you enjoy!"

He blinked at me, and said, *"...Why?"*

"Thought you were hungry. Let's go and get some air in the garden, ok?" I said.

We walked out to the garden, as the demon jumped whenever Beleth made any sort of noise, and looked out on stormy, desolate Hell, amidst the incorrigible plants in the garden, mostly Hellish weeds.

Dina offered the demon a cigarette, and he said, *"You are the old Queen. Thank you for your hospitality. I desire to serve your daughter for all eternity-"*

I asked him, "What else would you do, if you could also do that?"

He blinked at me, and said, *"I'd like some more chicken, please."*

I shrugged, and told a passing servant to get some more southern style chicken for our guest.

He blinked at me again.

We just sat enjoying Hell, and the demon made small talk, saying, *"I don't know why, but I've always enjoyed this sight. It's what I deserve."*

I said, "Yes, you do. But you also deserve to live in Hell like any normal person, if not a good person, then a morally grey person. You could just… eat chicken, and not worry about hurting and dominating slaves."

He blinked at me, and said, *"I do believe I've been workin' far too hard. I would like to go to the Gluttony Grill sometime. Always hear they have great food."*

I said, "They… do, so I'd love to go with you. I'm sure you'll see we can be friends, too."

He said, *"I think… I'd actually like that. I never had someone I would want to call a friend. I suppose it's not too late to start now."*

He sighed out.

He got more chicken, and burped, saying, "Excuse me, this is the best food I ever could've received, just like my slaves used to make."

I smiled to him, as he ate his chicken, a normal human.

74

Jane was petting Cerberus and playing with him, saying, "I've missed you so much, boy!! Don't get all nasty with *me* next time!!"

Cerberus whined, we petted him one last time, and waved him goodbye, going to Hana's castle.

The herald angel said, "Let's fly. I can see it in the distance, over there."

I said, "...But I don't know how to fly."

The herald angel said, "Oh well. Guess I'll carry you."

He grabbed my chest under the armpits from behind me, and took off from his eagle wings as I yelped, Yule flying on wings of white fire and Jane flying on black wings beside us.

We landed on a balcony, and I knocked on the door.

I heard Joli say, "...Is there a peeping Tom around here? Go away! Shoo!"

I heard Dominus say, "Maybe they'd like to join in. I know I would, if I was them."

Joli opened the door, a sheet around her naked body, and gasped in surprise, saying, "Oh! Tom! We needed you guys to bring Hana's baby away! Just let me get dressed."

She closed the door, and came back dressed in the shirt she got from her grandma and demon leather pants. I saw Dominus struggling with a pants leg as we followed Joli down to the Queen of Hell.

Yule said, as soon as we saw the blind Queen of Hell, Hanatrix, "It's been awhile, my niece."

"YULE! Ohgod, please, come here. Let me feel that scarred face of yours." Hana said.

Yule did, knelt before Hana sitting on her throne with a baby in her arm, and let Hana feel her face.

Hana sighed, and said, "As beautiful as always, Yule. I've missed you. And who are these two with the radiant presences? I know that's Tom in the back."

The herald angel said, "We've met once or twice, Hana… in a story of a dream…"

Hana smiled, and said, "Oh yes. I *do* remember you."

Jane shook Hana's hand, and said, "I see you've been doing a good job with this horrible, horrible place! I'm Mary Jane, call me Jane, and I was previously the Devil's Daughter, 'til I disowned myself."

Hana nodded at Jane, and said, "I've heard all sorts of stories about *you.* Well. get rid of the runt, and I can get back to work."

Hana tried handing the baby to Yule, but the baby just started crying and crying, looking like it would die again from oxygen loss, and Yule gave the baby back to Hana.

Hana sighed, and said, "Have you guys figured out why I'm getting *babies* now?"

I thought of something, as the baby was grasping so hard to Hana's hand.

I thought… What a pure soul, the both of them.

And then I realized that some of us, when we're lost and confused, cling to anything in the darkness…

Even if that be a blind woman who was Queen of Hell.

I said to Hana, "I… I think I know what to do, Hana. I think… you need to go to Heaven, or it is the fate of all the pure souls to be drawn to you."

A skinny woman said from the door, "Or you could come with me, my daughter."

75

Yule was gushing at her reunion with Dina again. Yule seemed to practically know everyone in the afterlife!

Dina said, "Not now, Yule dear. Allow Hana to make her choice."

Hana said, "B-But what do you mean, Tom? And Mom?"

Tom said, "These souls... look for the light, after death. And they find someone who will protect them no matter what, no matter who they are. They find you, Hana."

Dina said, "That they do. You can avoid this magnetism if you decide to go with me, to realms unseen. I miss a traveling companion at times, and who better to travel with than my daughter?"

Hana said, "You knew. You knew why this was happening, Mom..."

Dina said, "I knew you'd see the truth eventually."

Hana sighed, and said, "I... I don't want to lose you again... but I have so many people in this reality who I love, care for, and want to protect... But what will happen to Hell, if I leave?"

Beleth stepped up, bowed before Hana, and said, *"Do you wonder why I always bow to you, my Queen?"*

Hana said, "You do? I've never noticed."

Beleth said, *"I do. You have shown me a beautiful, fantastic piece of Hell, that I think I would like to continue for the time being. We could continue soul binding, with Joli teaching us when she can, and we can be... ourselves, as we like, for the first time. It chills me to the bones, such an opportunity..."*

Hana scowled, and said, "You like to talk a lot, but I think, as I have, I'll trust you on this. Joli, where do you want to go? I want to ask you, because you've been such a kind soul, a true friend to me, when I really haven't had any good friends in ages."

I smiled, and looked to Dominus, saying, "What do you want to do, lover?"

Dominus said, "Take the trip to Heaven, Joli. I... need to make up for some things, and will be going through Purgatory."

I kissed him, and said, "I'll wait for you."

Dominus seemed so relaxed, Beleth grinned in anticipation, and Dina gave her daughter a big hug.

She said, "I promise I'll visit you again, Hana. There are so many... stories, I must live, before I do, though."

Hana hugged her back close, I blinked, and Dina had disappeared.

The herald angel said, "Well. Let's go up, everyone. Jane, grab the baby, Yule, pick up Hana, and Tom, grab Joli, and everyone, just don't drop them. Dominus, I'll give you a free lift to Purgatory, free of charge, Heaven style."

Dominus smiled, and accepted the ride.

Tom looked confused.

76

I said, "How... I can't fly, I don't know how to fly!" to Joli.

Joli just smiled, and said, "I believe in you, Tom. You know how to fly."

I looked into her eyes, and nodded. She jumped into my arms, after we all went outside, and... I looked up.

Straight. Up.

I thought of my wife, telling me every time before a show, "You can do it."

I thought of the herald angel, giving me a job I learned to love.

I thought of God, and all his fantastic people, waiting for me with open arms up above.

And I... I flew.

I flew, even though I had no wings.

We circled each other through the sky of Hell, and got to Purgatory.

The herald angel dropped Dominus off with Paul, and Dominus blew Joli kisses in my arms, waving us goodbye for a while.

And we kept flying up.

Straight into the wide open, blue sky.

Through the clouds, around and around.

And through all of magnificent creation.

We got to the gates, and St. Peter let us in, and I let Joli go.

Joli, the soul binder, kissed me on the cheek, and said, "I'm so glad we met, Tom, wing fitter."

We ambled back to Heaven, where all our friends were waiting, and even God, with a big, friendly smile.

I asked the herald angel what about his car. He said it had already been scrapped years ago.

And God said…

And we all lived happily ever after.

77

Beleth's Epilogue

Hello. This is the resolution part of the story, the part where you get to feel oh so happy that everything continues to turn out right for the main characters. But what about poor Beleth?

I was eating at the Gluttony Grill, only a light portion of evil food for me, all sorts of sinful concoctions that would keep you eternally thirsty and hungry, never sated, but I had an upset stomach that day.

And I was surrounded by the archdemons of deadly sin.

Belphegor, guardian of sloth, Asmodeus, guardian of lust, Beelzebub, guardian of gluttony, Mammon, guardian of greed, Leviathan, guardian of envy, and oh, whatever I'll be a guardian of wrath, and I had the guardian of pride, Satan, in a grocery bag by my side. Humans get our jobs messed up all the time, in fact we trade jobs with each other constantly just for fun and to confuse them. Really, when thinking of a demon, all you have to do is remember one thing...

We're bad news.

It was very pleasant being a butler, and I have a happy sigh coming out of me whenever I think back on those days... but now, I was Hell's eternal ruler, and all must feel my wrath (thus the guardian of wrath bit.)

I just had to make these demons see me as their overlord, seducing, bribing, stealing, or extorting their power from them. Yes, even the burning book called Satan. He's the only one who would STILL try and maintain his "superiority" over us, despite really only being a burning paperweight, and some demons respect him for that.

The burning book, who was in fact slow cooking my turkey in the grocery bag, said, "Why can't Molech be the guardian of wrath? He was a great leader, a brute of a monster... Quite loyal, as well..."

The other demons murmured affirmations to this, playing into Satan's measly power play. This in fact was a way to undermine my authority, and keep power split amongst us. Satan did this ploy for years... but all we got out of it was a wasteland of Hell. I learned, through serving my two past Queens, that we can accomplish much grander feats with unified powers and goals.

I politely said, "Molech has shown his true face, that he is a useless rebel, to anyone who wishes to claim power. I prefer him trapped as a statue, and his despicably weak fight against angels in the living world, where he failed continuously, shows that he is not worthy of such a title."

The other demons murmured affirmations, even Satan, Satan saying, "Well, yes. He got roughhoused by a few kids who happened to be slightly supernatural."

My own power play. I defended my own worthless "title," making my, and therefore their, positions seem petty in comparison to me. I was the one who held a lot of past power, and without these pesky titles I'd have claimed complete authority in a manner of moments.

Leviathan said, "I wish I had your job, Beleth... You got lucky. Why should we allow you in this council? You obviously bow low before any, even pure souls and humans."

Leviathan always had the little green gremlin in his skin. But some, who are touched by envy, think that if they cannot have something, then no one should, thus his distaste for me.

Beelzebub, whose restaurant I always promoted, said, "Hey now, Beleth's been living the good life. Any of us would take a nice break like that, if we could. Souls to torture, right hand position... I only ask one thing, Beleth. Why didn't you do more? We could've aided you."

They murmured, not all in affirmation. Some were just murmuring.

I said, "I did all I could for you, dear demons. For all of you. You've noticed, that you were all allowed off from the Queen's," (and therefore my) "wrath quite noticeably. Except for you, Asmodeus, and I am quite sorry you only dug your way out of the dirt today."

Asmodeus grumbled, a past boyfriend of Hana's that she wanted to bury and forget about for an eternity, literally in Asmodeus's case. Asmodeus said, "I just really gotta find something to fuck. I don't care what, and I really don't care about this little charade of a council. You'll all see, even if we fight each other, it feels good to do what you really want to do after we're done enacting justice on each other."

Hmm. Asmodeus, playing the peacemaker. Well, there's only one demon who knows what to do to a peacemaker... and he would try to deceive him.

Satan said, "Quite right. Now let me out of this book and we can all go get drunk again. All of you... my crowning, rebellious angels... Let's forget about the past."

Belphegor said, "I'd rather do this tomorrow, honestly."

They were murmuring in agreeal to Satan's proposal, but I thankfully had a nice leverage on Satan, for all time.

I said, "Sorry, Satan, but as you know... No one knows how to bring you out of the book, besides Dina, the one who put you in it."

The other demons hmmed, as Satan grumbled in anger. He knew the truth of this, but as always thought I held out on him important information. I usually do, and actually I was holding this fact for when I could use it most. No one knew how to free Satan. Even Hana tried in a theoretical scenario, but it was impossible for her as well.

Mammon bluntly said, "I will buy all of your positions, power, whatever, from you, and you can all do whatever you like, for all time."

The demons were silent. Belphegor broke silence first, and said, "So you mean I get to laze around, not work, and FINALLY relax?"

Mammon said, "Of course. You'll have credit with every shop in Hell, every DEMON in Hell, and can do whatever you want to them-"

Asmodeus said, "...Whatever... I want?"

Mammon said, "Whatever you want."

Mammon was a difficult case, silently swaying the economy, which Hana needed running all throughout Hell. She always undercut his power where she could, but no one can outfinance a guardian of greed...

Asmodeus and Belphegor placed their pieces of archdemon souls on the table, which Mammon gathered up, and which Mammon traded them each a golden credit card of infinite worth. The two went to fuck and sleep forever, and would never be satisfied for the rest of their eternity because of it.

Leviathan said, "I want both. I want those, and I want that credit card."

The two stared daggers into each other, and Beelzebub said, "Come, don't bicker like children. Let us make a new pact, with those two idiots out of the picture. Let us conjoin the wealth, and be equal rulers of Hell."

Ahh. Now we were talking about what we really wanted.

Mammon squinted at Beelzebub, and Leviathan said, "Yes. I want that too. I just want that. I would be willing to share... as long as I have it."

Mammon said, "I think I've seen enough. You all cannot make any headway without me, and I-"

This is where one of my "improvements" to Hell came in.

I said, "I propose a new economy, inspired to me from the soul binder, Joli. Instead of trading useless specks of OTHER souls, we trade for our OWN. I'm sure all of you, like me, have given up pieces of your soul here and there. This way power remains checked, and we continue to better our people."

Mammon gasped, and Leviathan said, "...I could have a pure soul again? My OWN? I want that the most. You've got my vote for supreme leader, Beleth. If you can give me a piece, just somewhere to start..."

I sighed, and said, "So pitiful, Leviathan, you have my sympathies. I did find a remnant," (just in case stored for an eternity by me) "in the old Queen's chambers. Here you are, Leviathan. Use your soul well."

I then handed Leviathan a bright light, and Leviathan gasped as he felt his soul slightly reconverge.

He smiled at me, and left the restaurant.

Mammon said, "I won't hear of this. I'll be working against this system all the way, know this, Beleth, demon of MUSIC, you've made a powerful enemy..."

Beelzebub could smell, like in his restaurant, a wafting, enticing allure of power. I desired he come no where near my new system, but he allied himself with me and said, "What if we allowed you, Mammon, to create a corporation of soul binders? I'm sure Beleth's would love to teach the new workforce, and you would be top of the market, maybe not in souls, but in our other wealth."

Mammon rubbed his chin, and said, "Deal. As long as she comes straight away to me. Good day... gentlemen."

Mammon put on his tophat, and left the scene.

Well. We now had a new economy, and a brand new workforce of devoted soul binders. And there were two demons left at the table, and a burning book in my grocery bag.

Beelzebub said, "What's with the groceries, Beleth?"

I said, "I'm making dinner for Joli coming by. Just pleasantries, I assure you, and then she can get to work and teach demons to bind their souls."

Beelzebub said, "You would rather not come here? You and her are always welcome."

I smiled, and said, "I prefer to eat somewhere Joli hasn't thrown up at. She has great taste."

Beelzebub said, "Was there... something between you two?"

I said, "Hm? Oh god no. You're making me lose my appetite. Just friends, I assure you."

"...You wouldn't... be in the market to sell her, would you? All of her." Beelzebub said.

I hmmed, and said, "For what? What can you give me?"

"...Eternal power. You've been doing great work, Beleth, but... you always come up short, especially on tips. Trade her to me, in an act of good faith, and I assure you we will rise... To Heaven, to the living world, all realms..." Beelzebub said.

"Enticing. That IS what I've dreamed of for all of my creation..." I said.

"And I'm sure the soul binder can help us." he said.

"You, you mean. I would love to trade her, if I could get anything out of her... but you are weak, Beelzebub, thus your place in Hell.

"I understand my weakness, thus I understand servitude. I understand the power of others', thus I understand my own.

"And I know this... You are weak, Beelzebub. I'd like some more ketchup, if that would be ok. I promise to leave you a nice tip." I said.

Beelzebub was pale in anger, but slowly, went to get me my ketchup.

I ate my meal, and the burning book said, "...Quite well done, Beleth. Just like this turkey. What are you going to do with me?"

"I don't really know. Does anyone? Can you still do that trick of switching chapters? Would be a nice prank to play on Joli." I said.

Satan sighed, and said, "Yes..."

"Good. I expect you to inspire her, entertain her, and all the likes a good book should do. You must accept your role, Satan, and realize... books are a blessing. They can do so much for a person, and yet still be so little. Be a good book, Satan." I said.

Satan said yes, and I paid my check, leaving a nice tip, and left the restaurant.

I walked back home to the castle, my now supreme castle of command, and looked up at the sun shining down on me pleasantly.

"Gosh. What a sight. Like being in Heaven." I said, whistling down the road.

www.ingramcontent.com/pod-product-compliance
Lightning Source LLC
LaVergne TN
LVHW010201070526
838199LV00062B/4451
9798985568578